HIS FIRE MAIDEN

SPACE LORDS: A QURILIXEN WORLD NOVEL

MICHELLE M. PILLOW

MICHELLE M. PILLOW® - MICHELLEPILLOW.COM

Space Lords: His Fire Maiden

© Copyright 2016-2018, Michelle M. Pillow

Second Printing July 2018, The Raven Books LLC

First Printing Jan 2016

ISBN 978-1-62501-417-7

Published by The Raven Books LLC

To all the wonderful people who've made The Raven Books LLC a success: the editors, artists, authors, distributors, my bestie Mandy M. Roth, and especially the awesome readers who keep coming back for more. Without you, I couldn't be doing what I love.

And for those like Violette who enjoy stepping just a little too close to the flame.

SPACE LORDS SERIES

His Frost Maiden
His Fire Maiden
His Metal Maiden
His Earth Maiden
His Woodland Maiden

ABOUT THE BOOK

Dev has found a home with a misfit outlaw band of space pirates and he will do anything to protect his makeshift family. He knows he will never be accepted into human society. The demonic race of his birth shuns him and the humans fear him. So when the woman of his dreams comes gunning for his crew, the fiery maiden leaves him no choice but to show just how naughty his demon can be.

Series Note: Part of the Dragon Lords World

WELCOME TO QURILIXEN

Qurilixen World Novels

Dragon Lords Series
Barbarian Prince
Perfect Prince
Dark Prince
Warrior Prince
His Highness The Duke
The Stubborn Lord
The Reluctant Lord
The Impatient Lord
The Dragon's Queen

Dynasty Lords Series
Seduction of the Phoenix
Temptation of the Butterfly

To learn more about the Qurilixen World series of
books and to stay up to date on the latest book list
visit www.MichellePillow.com

AUTHOR UPDATES

To stay informed about when a new book in the
series installments is released, sign up for updates:

http://michellepillow.com/author-updates/

NOTE FROM THE AUTHOR

Author recommends reading book one, His Frost Maiden. Though not necessary to this book, it does give a lot of the characters' back-stories.

Dear Readers,

I'm pleased to present you with the next installment of my ongoing series, *Space Lords*. These books continue the best-selling *Dragon Lords*, *Lords of the Var®*, and *Zhang Dynasty* series. For those of you catching up on the Dragon Lords World, a complete reading order list is available on my website, michellepillow.com. Though they can be read alone, I recommend reading books in order of release for full enjoyment.

There are several themes in *Space Lords 2: His*

Fire Maiden, which are carried over from previous titles. First is Zhang An's curse on the crewmen from *Lords of the Var® 5: The Pirate Prince*. Second is the dynamic between Josselyn Craven (*Space Lords 1: His Frost Maiden*) and Violette Craven Stephans. To fully understand the complete dynamic between Violette and Josselyn, I recommend reading *His Frost Maiden*. Here is a quick summary to get you up to speed:

About Violette and Josselyn…

In short, Josselyn was horribly wronged by General Jack Stephans, Violette's father. Over a hundred years ago, Jack's betrayal caused the destruction of Josselyn's home world and the death of everyone in her family except for Lady Craven, her mother. As a small act of mercy toward Josselyn, Jack had her imprisoned in a stone-like state, keeping her in stasis until she was released in *His Frost Maiden*.

Lady Craven, being of a very delicate nature, never knew of Jack's involvement. She married the general, the only thing left from her destroyed past. Together, they had Violette. Lady Craven died in childbirth. Physically, Josselyn and Violette are around the same age, even though Josselyn was born over a hundred years before her half-sister.

Jack, in an act of contrition, has spent his life as

an alienitarian and humanitarian to atone for past mistakes. This is the father Violette knows. This is the man whose death she believes she must avenge. Josselyn is her target. Violette does not know of Josselyn's past nor her true connection to Jack.

About The Zhang Curse...

The Conqueror pilot, Rick Hayes has always had a big mouth—one that often gets him into trouble. Such is the case when Captain Jarek goes to ask Princess Zhang Mei's parents for her hand in marriage at the Imperial Palace (Book: *Lords of the Var® 5: The Pirate Prince*). Ancestral spirits roam the palace, but none is so involved with the living as Zhang An. An prides herself on her ability to not only see the future, but to manipulate the living with her cryptic visions.

Mei's parents weren't thrilled with the way she went about finding a husband, or her desire to leave their home planet. As tensions rose, Rick decided to step in and draw attention from the couple to himself. It was a sweet, if slightly misguided gesture of loyalty on his part. His interference, combined with his natural ability to put his foot in his mouth drew An's anger. Instead of just bringing the ancestral Zhang spirit's curse upon himself, Rick caused her wrath to turn to the other members of Captain Jarek's crew—at least those unfortunate enough to be present at the time. Rick really is a good man. He'd give his life for any one of his friends, just as they would give their life for him. But caring for the man like a brother doesn't change the fact that he can be downright infuriating at times.

Cursed crewmen include: Evan, Dev, Jackson, Lochlann, Rick

Thank you for your continual support of the Dragon Lords World.

Happy Reading!

Michelle

CHAPTER 1

PROLOGUE

RIFFLEN FEDERATION MILITARY BASE, Desert Planet of Rifflen, V Quadrant

Violette Craven Stephans stared as the blood trailed down her forearm over her hand, only to watch as it dripped steadily from her fingertips onto the hard tile floor by her feet. For a long moment the deliberate cut didn't even hurt, but then a deep pain radiated over her, and she cried out as she moved to pull the limb close to her body in a protective gesture.

"This is a blood oath, Violette, between us." Her father grabbed her wrist and shook it hard, forcing her eyes to meet his steely green ones. His fingers slipped in her blood as he held too tight. "I need you to remember this moment. I need you to remember what I tell you. And I need you never to speak of it to anyone."

Violette was still too stunned by the fact that her father had actually cut her to give him a quick answer. In all of her eight years, she had never seen her father angry with her, let alone violent enough to do her harm. What made it all the more puzzling is that she hadn't been doing anything wrong—at least, she didn't think she had been. It wasn't like the time she had burrowed a tiny hole in the military base's transparent exterior wall because she wanted some sand from outside. The entire military structure was located beneath the moving white dunes of Rifflen's sandy surface. That one hole caused a pressure crack that could have caved in and buried the four hundred and sixteen residents of the base. For that she'd been stuck in room seclusion for a mere two days.

"Your blood is mine, and mine is yours," he continued. "Do you understand? If you do not honor your word, nothing in your life will matter for you will have forsaken your blood. Do you understand me? Blood is everything."

Her father, General Jack Stephans, was an important man—not just because he was her father, a general in the Federation Military, and the sole authority on the Rifflen base, but because he was a humanitarian and an alienitarian. He dedicated much of his life to promoting equality and fairness between alien races.

"The universes are a big place," he would tell people. *"Large enough to hold all species. Humanoids are no better than a Kintok, or a Torg, or a…"*

"Do you understand?" he repeated, louder than before, shaking her from her scattered thoughts. The smell of liquor was thick on his breath.

She looked from his eyes to her blood and then back again, trying to reconcile what she knew with what had just happened. Frightened, she nodded. The fear she felt of him at that moment outweighed the physical pain caused by his thin blade. Her fingers tingled with numbness. In truth, she didn't understand. "I only wanted to watch the new holo-box. It didn't say it was military access only. It didn't need a code to view it. I thought it would be one of your species profiles or an award invitation. You always let me see them."

The holo-box was a standard issue Federation communication device, initially used to send encoded memos and official orders. Now, they were utilized by the military for all sorts of formal letters, when more than a voice was needed. Private messages were always encrypted so that the wrong person couldn't watch them.

Instead of an award, the holographic recording had shown the small image of her father, standing in his shiny white uniform on the round disc on top of the box. It appeared as if it had been recorded that very morning. He'd been talking about some strange things too, things that didn't make any sense to her child brain.

"Josselyn, I'm glad you are well," the recording had said. *"It's what I've hoped for these last, long years. By this time and because you are still alive after the term of your imprisonment has ended, we have probably spoken. Knowing the temperament of your family, we have not spoken kindly. So much has happened and changed since that day long ago, and I have to force myself to remember that you don't know the good I've tried to do. All you know is my sins. I cannot take back that which was done, but I can give you a new life. With these papers, you will never have to explain your age or your past. As my daughter, a general's daughter, you will have the freedom to pass by Federation ports unhampered. I cannot leave the life I have chosen. The Federation has granted me the home, which I so longed to be a part of in those years you knew me as a reward for my services. I know it is not the land it once was, but all it is, I give to you."*

Her father looked at his desk and frowned. His grip on her arm loosened, and she pulled her wrist free. She took a slow step back, careful not to make too many sudden movements. Her eyes darted to the thick oak door of her father's private office. The wood seemed out of place in the metal construct of the military base. Carved patterns spoke of craftsmanship and time, not portability and ease of assembly. A barren fireplace graced one wall, surrounded by emblems and even a banner with the Craven family crest. Craven had been her mother's title and name, a title her father had taken when they married, a title that would be passed on to her—the *only* child of the couple. Her mother had died soon after she was born. All Violette had were the memories and descriptions her father had given her. That title was her gift from her mother. The name, a few holographic images, a notion, and a family crest—that was Violette's mother's legacy. How could her father think to give any Craven land to this Josselyn woman?

Violette's legs trembled, as she was unsure what to make of her father's expression. His shortly cropped black-gray hair and hard green eyes appeared both menacing and familiar. He wore his white, long tunic uniform, material that gleamed as it reflected the soft orange firelight. A thin brown stripe ran down the sides of his legs and arms, signifying his rank. Her clothing mimicked his in style though the loose pants and tunic were blue and cut with shorter sleeves.

"Who is Josselyn? Why did you call her your daughter?" Her eyes filled with tears. Violette didn't have siblings. "I don't understand. Why would you give her your land? I'm your daughter. Me! My mother died after giving birth to me. You said—"

"There are things you cannot understand," he whispered. "Things you cannot comprehend. The land I spoke of does not belong to you. You will never see it." Then louder, his eyes clearing as he found her inching away from him in fear, he added, "You *must* promise me you will not say a word about what you have seen, and promise that you will not interfere in this matter because—"

"Who is she?" Violette demanded, dying to discover the answer. She had never seen his eyes so cold.

"There are things you don't understand, Violette!" Then, softening his demeanor, as if the gesture took great effort on his part, he continued, "You are my daughter. My blood daughter. As my heir, you will be well taken care of. The land I speak of is not for you. You would not want it. All that you see here is yours, including what is in my safe. Always remember that this base operates on the old code, and you will not be questioned, or stopped from taking what is yours. You will always be provided for. I have seen to it."

"I remember the old code," she said softly. "I won't forget."

"Good girl." He gave her a small nod. "That is why this oath is important because I know you will not be able to break your word to me. Someday, a woman named Josselyn might attempt to find me. She's my history, my personal ghost, and she's a furious one. You must not get in her way. Whatever she comes to do, you must promise me you will not try to stop her. What will come is what must be, for events were put into motion long before you were born."

Her father rolled the sleeve of his shiny, pristine uniform and reached for his knife, holding it gingerly in his palm.

"What else did the holo-box say? You didn't let it finish," she interrupted what he was doing. She pulled her bleeding arm closer to her stomach. The blood wet her shirt, but she didn't care.

His eyes moved briefly to where the holo-box sat on his desk next to a stack of ID chips, intergalactic maps, and official travel papers. When he again looked at her, he'd banished the anger from his grave expression. "Promise me that when Josselyn comes, you will not interfere. Someday you will be a great captain, heir to my fortune and to my position on this base should you choose that path. But, blood is thicker than military ranking. Promise me, when Josselyn comes, you will obey my wishes and not lift a finger to stop what she chooses to do. You will let events play out as they are meant to regardless of the cost."

"I don't understand," Violette protested, puzzled. Her father lifted his knife and sliced through his arm. Without giving her a choice, he lunged forward and grabbed her, placing her cut to his to bind the wounds together. Their blood mingled on her skin, and she felt dizzy. The acrid odor seemed all at once overwhelming and comforting.

"Your blood has made the oath for you. The scar you are left with will remind you of the promise, but I would have you say the words. Say you promise. You will not ask about Josselyn again. You will not speak of my history unless I speak of her first. And, when the time comes, if I ask you to do something, to help her, you will do what I say without question and without hesitation. Do you understand me? Say you promise."

"I promise." Violette nodded, and her father released her arm.

"Good girl. Good." He suddenly seemed despondent. The general stood for a long moment, staring at his wound. "I am sorry you looked at the box, Violette, thus making this necessary. I wished for you never to have known."

She backed away from him, wanting nothing more than to run to the furthest corner of the military base. There was no escaping the enclosed building beneath the moving white sands, but she knew every secret hiding spot, every tight corner.

Her father turned from her and lifted a decanter to pour himself a drink. "Before you go to your virtual flying lesson see the medic and have your cut attended to, but leave the scar. I will not have you forgetting your promise."

CHAPTER 2

IMPERIAL PALACE of the Zhang Dynasty, Planet of Lintian, Many years later…

"Holy space balls," Rick Hayes swore as he reached forward to poke his finger into the transparent elderly woman floating next to him. The spirit turned and arched her brow in annoyance. When she moved away from him, dark hair streaked with white lifted around her head unhampered by gravity, and her long sleeves drifted in the breeze.

Dev tried not to let his grimace show. It appeared the Imperial Palace was infested with ancestral spirits. Actual ghosts were rare occurrences. In fact, many cultures didn't believe they even existed. He'd seen several milling about though he pretended not to since no one else had indicated they knew the apparitions were there…until Rick's run in with this mysterious elemental lady.

Blast it all!

Dev had been on enough high skies adventures to know things generally did not end well when Rick became curious. The pilot's big mouth was sure to drop them into trouble again, and it would be Dev's duty to make sure he pulled them out of it. He owed Rick his life. If Captain Samantha's crew hadn't saved him and made him part of their family, he'd be nothing but a crispy memory told by a Data Moon Base Brimstoneman.

Rarely had he felt such desperation and fear, as he had the day he was almost sacrificed. Bad wiring had compromised Dev's vessel, and his shields had given out during entry into Data Moon Base's atmosphere. The local zealots saw the flaming ball of his ship zipping to the ground near their Earth Settlement and naturally assumed it was a special delivery from the devil.

Yeah, Dev thought sarcastically, *because what would be more likely? The legendary devil cared enough to attack a fanatical orb of a dust ball world, or a transporter ship had malfunctioned and had to make an emergency landing?*

Luckily, Dev's Bevlon blood had kept him from burning up during reentry. Not so fortunately, that same blood had also almost gotten him skinned and set on fire. In his nightmares he could still hear a young boy's hateful chanting, *"Into the fire! Into the flame! Burn him now and feel no shame!"*

Dev knew how he appeared to many humanoid cultures. One look and they wanted him dead, all because he had been born Salebinaben Johobik en Dehauberkelsain en Thoraxian en Yyrtolzx Devekin. His father had been full-blooded Bevlon, a demonic-like race in appearance. His mother had been human. The fruition of his parents' strange relationship had produced Dev. It was his red skin and dark eyes that had set the Data Moon zealots off. He'd inherited the intense coloring, large body size, and black eyes and hair from his father. The humanlike form he'd received from his mother.

"Burn him! Listen to the angel and burn the demon spawn!"

"Crucify him!"

"Burn the demon!"

The voices were etched deep into his memory. Dev hadn't expected to be rescued. Back then, no one cared whether he lived or died. Bevlons did not coddle their children into adulthood, and he didn't know his human mother.

His loyalty to Rick and the others was from more than the fact they'd saved him, an outsider no one else cared about. The crew had become some-thing Dev had never imagined he would have—a real family. Sure, Rick was like the pesky little brother he sometimes wanted to throw into deep space without a suit, but no one else better try it.

Remembering the past helped Dev stay focused in the present, but more importantly it reminded him why he wasn't dragging Rick from the palace by his hair. Rick made another move toward the spirit. Dev focused a glare of warning in the man's direction and gave a small shake of his head. Rick winked back at him.

Dev had been alone until Captain Samantha and her band of misfits came for him, a condemned stranger. Crewman and empath Evan Cormier had seen Dev in one of his visions. Rick, Samantha, and Evan had come in with laser pistols blasting while the brothers, Lucien and Viktor, had waited with the ship ready to make their getaway.

Dev would give his life to protect his makeshift family. They accepted him, teased him, baited him, and, yes, occasionally called him Barbecue Boy, but they would put themselves on the line to save him. Together they traveled from adventure to adventure, wherever their ship landed. Recently, Samantha had married a cat-shifter and was now settled on the man's home planet of Qurilixen. It did not change their bond, and Dev would always answer her call if she needed him.

His new captain, Jarek, was Samantha's brother-by-marriage. The man had offered them a place on his ship. He needed to replenish his depleted crew, and they needed a purpose. Jarek and his men were all honorable, even if they were borderline space pirates.

Jarek's second-in-command, Lochlann, was a dragon-shifter. The men came from the same home planet. The two were long-time friends who had run away from home because dragon-shifters and cat-shifters were at war. Neither one of them had wanted to fight, so they chose the high skies. Though the war on Qurilixen was over, the men's families didn't fully accept their friendship.

Lastly, there was Jackson, a highly trained super soldier. To Dev, the man was a kindred spirit. He had the same drive and determination, and the almost compulsive need to train for battle in the Virtual Reality room aboard their ship.

This was Dev's life. It was more than a half-demon reject could have ever hoped to achieve. He did not dare aspire to have more. And it was how he found himself in a royal alien palace silently praying Rick would not sexually proposition an old lady's ghost.

One would think escorting Princess Mei to visit her family wouldn't demand a quick departure off planet. Then again, *One* wouldn't know Rick's penchant for mischief in any situation.

They stood inside the Hall of Infinite Wisdom

located in the center of the palace compound. The building was a large structure, set high upon stone to tower over the surrounding courtyard and gardens. If the ornate décor was any indication, the local royals had lived in isolation for some time, away from any kind of real intergalactic conflict.

Dev stayed toward the back of those gathered to keep an eye on everyone. He didn't like their odds of escape from inside the belly of the fortified palace, but bad odds didn't mean impossible. There were numerous official reasons why they had come to the planet, but really it was so Jarek could ask for Mei's parents' blessing to marry her. Since, technically, the crew had kidnapped Mei to begin with, it wasn't likely her parents would be too excited by the proposal.

Evan crossed his arms over his chest and kept his attention on the Emperor and Empress. Dev wasn't sure if Evan was trying to read the royals, or trying not to, so he watched the man for a sign that all was not well. Evan did not like using his ability, but would if necessity called for it. Returning a kidnapped princess to angry parents with an army at their fingertips might warrant such a necessity.

Like a child with a new toy, Rick couldn't seem to help himself. He ran his hand into the apparition's upper leg. "She feels like air."

Mei turned at Rick's words and eyed the situation. She nodded toward the spirit, and quickly introduced, "This is my great-grandmother, Zhang An. She is my ancestor who helps to watch over and guide us," before continuing her somewhat private conversation with her parents and Jarek.

Rick made a move to touch An again and the spirit silently glided out of his reach. An was clearly aware of what was happening but chose to ignore Rick as she focused on her living relatives. Dev let loose a captured breath as it appeared the crisis might be averted.

Dev shared a quick look with Jackson. The man leaned toward him and whispered, "Should we grab Rick before he does something really foolish?"

"Next time I vote we lock him on board the ship." Dev studied the locals, trying to judge their temperament. He had a feeling one word from the Emperor would produce a significant number of trained guards. Part of him wanted the fight. It might be a fun challenge. Then again, he wouldn't want to put the others in harm's way.

"Mei belongs with the captain," Jackson whispered. "If they don't approve, we take her by force. Look at how they act toward her and then watch her expression. She does not belong here. If only we would be so lucky to find—"

"Jackson, you have to feel her," Rick interrupted softly. He had stepped close to the spirit once more. "I swear, it's like she's not even there, but she is."

Jackson made a move to grab Rick as if he'd forcibly pull him from the room. Dev placed his hand on his arm to stop him. "This is the captain's future. Let him handle it how he sees fit." Observing a servant looking into the room from a doorway across the hall, Dev nodded to direct Jackson's attention to her.

"If Rick's ass gets thrown into a local prison for feeling up a dead woman, I'm not going after him." Jackson kept an eye on the servant until she disappeared. Dev knew it was a lie. Jackson would be the first one to volunteer for the mission.

As Mei began to argue about her future happiness with the ancestral spirit and her parents, Dev felt sorry for Jarek. Dev couldn't imagine having a woman to love. He long ago accepted he was not meant for such things. After years of being ridiculed and feared as a demon, he was used to people trying to attack him without reason or provocation. What sane woman would want a half-breed devil in her bed, let alone in her heart? If the Emperor thought Jarek was unworthy of his daughter, Dev could only imagine what would have happened had a demon stood in the captain's place.

"She should marry the father of her unborn

child," An declared in support of Mei leaving with Jarek.

That caught Dev's attention. Mei was pregnant out of wedlock? Her parents didn't seem too pleased by the news. They stared at the couple in shock. The Emperor looked ready to call his guards.

"Oh, blasted spaceholes," Jackson swore. His entire body tensed. "Get ready."

Dev waited, carefully watching the Emperor for a sign of attack.

"Way to go, Cap!" Rick yelled suddenly, breaking the awkward silence as he drew the heated attention toward himself. "You sent off some straight shooters right up the ole—"

"Rick," Dev growled, unable to take the man's nonsense a second longer. He grabbed him to shut him up.

"Ow, let go," Rick demanded. "*I* didn't knock her up."

Dev released him, realizing a second too late that Rick knew exactly what he was doing. The man only acted the way he did to pull negative attention away from the captain and his pregnant lover. In comparison to Rick, Jarek would look like an exceptional choice. Also, if everyone was staring at Rick, the lovers would be able to make a run for it if they so chose.

The ploy worked. An turned on Rick to keep

the attention off Mei and Jarek. "You insolent little..."

"Whoa, easy there, ghostly sweetness, you'll get your chance at me," Rick said, grinning at the older woman. "No need to call Dev names."

The bad joke was Rick's attempt to defuse the situation he'd created. An's figure shuddered with light and her face tinted with pink. Furious, she pointed at him, "I will teach you respect, little man. You will bow in the presence of my greatness."

Rick paled, apparently realizing that he'd played his asinine role too well. "Hey, now, I was just joking around. Things were getting a little tense, and I was just trying to save the captain from everyone's anger. You know, lightening the mood with humor."

"Do not make me curse you," An warned.

"Rick, I'd listen to her and say no more," Evan interjected.

"Easy, don't get your, uh, gown in a twist," Rick said, ignoring Evan's sensible advice. Though he was great at causing trouble, he wasn't the best at calming it. "No need to threaten us with whatever mojo power thing you have."

Jackson hit Rick's arm. "Shut your black hole."

"Ah, so you think you are funny?" An's eyes glazed with white. "Let's see how humorous you and your friends think my power is."

Jarek started to take a step forward to protect his

men. Dev awaited his command. Mei pulled Jarek back, shaking her head. "She predicts their future. No physical harm will come to them."

An's voice took on an ominous quality. "Together you travel, and together you'll remain. Tied and joined like the five elements of our people. The road to happiness is very rocky for all of you."

"What does that mean?" Lochlann whispered. It was the first he'd spoken since they'd walked into the palace hall.

"Is she telling the truth?" Jackson questioned Evan, as if skeptical of the ghost's powers.

"I don't know," Evan answered. "I can't read spirits."

"Great going, space cadet." Jackson nudged Rick.

An's eyes cleared, and she smiled vindictively, evidently knowing something they didn't. "You will find your love hidden within the mystery of the five elements. One element for each of you." She moved her eyes over Lochlann, Evan, Dev, Jackson, and Rick. "The corresponding element will hold the secret to your future happiness. But fate is not clear. If you do not recognize it, you will lose it and be forever alone."

"Elements?" Lochlann repeated. "What elements?"

"Yes. The secret of your future is hidden in the five elements—metal, water, wood, earth, and fire."

"Which one am I?" Jackson asked.

"And I?" Lochlann questioned.

"That is for you to figure out." With that, An blew away on a sudden gust of wind. Dev watched her leave the hall. Seeing her ineloquently saunter away when she thought the living could no longer see her did take away some of her scary mystery vibe.

"How does predicting what will come curse us?" Rick frowned.

"She just gives us enough to consume our thoughts," Evan said. "Trust me, knowing only a very small piece of something will drive you mad. The thought will creep into our heads and make us crazy."

"Metal, wood..." Lochlann tried to recite.

"Water, earth, fire," Evan finished.

"Dev's got fire, that's easy," Rick said. "And I must be metal because my body is rock hard with muscles."

"I think the elements refer to the ones we are meant for," Evan said. "Not who we are."

"She didn't say that," Rick protested. "I'm metal. I know it."

Dev didn't speak. There was nothing for him to say. It was as if she'd found the one secret weapon that could hurt him and stabbed him with it—the desire to be loved and accepted. A physical ache filled his chest, so he held himself rigid and waited for the pain to pass. He knew he was not meant to find love, but to have it dangled before him so unexpectedly was most brutal. His hand clenched. He wanted to punch Rick. He wanted to chase after An and make her tell him more. For if he had a chance at losing love, then that meant there was actually a chance he would someday find it. That hope was the cruelest part of all.

And maybe the whole curse thing was just a mean prank told by a cranky spirit, and nothing had really changed.

CHAPTER 3

RIFFLEN FEDERATION MILITARY BASE, Several Months Later

"Back away. That is the general's heart alarm. He's dying." Captain Violette pushed past the men who were rushing toward the general's door. They couldn't do anything for him, not if his heart alarm was already sounding. She hurried to be by her father's side, hoping in vain to make it in those last seconds of his life. When she'd obeyed his order to escort the mysterious Josselyn safely onto the base, she never expected the woman would dare to murder him in his own office. Why would she? He was giving Josselyn land, travel papers, and credentials. Why would she kill him?

Violette's stomach tightened. Time appeared to slow as she strode toward the office door. Part of her had been waiting for this day for the last thirty years, since he'd made her promise an oath over their bloody arms, but she never thought it would result in his death. Her father was so healthy, so good, so...

Dead?

The base's alarm repeated in a series of two short beeps and one long. Violette ignored it. She didn't want to be here. She wanted to rewind time, back to the moment when Josselyn approached her on the floating bucket of asteroid dust they called a fuel dock out in the middle of deep space. She should have disobeyed her father. She should have insisted on being in the room with the two of them. Already she knew it was too late. Her father was gone. There were no last seconds to be had with him. Not with the alarm. The death notice was being automatically sent out to the Federation.

Her father hadn't talked about Josselyn since the day Violette found the holo-box—until a few weeks ago when he simply told her it was time. It would appear her father's mystery lady was real—*very real* —and, by the look of her, too young to have plagued her father's conscience as long as she had. Josselyn looked to be Violette's age, maybe even younger, but had been born when her father was a very young man, which made her closer to a hundred. If Violette hadn't known about the Federation's short stint preserving prisoners into a stone-like state, she would have wondered at the clear discrepancy in the timeline.

Violette kept moving. She didn't let her panic or grief show. The general wouldn't have wanted her to display weakness. As she touched the door, she said to the soldiers, "You have your orders. As his heir, I'm in charge now until the Federation sends his replacement. This base operates on the old codes, and I invoke my rights."

She walked into her father's office, and the sick feeling intensified. Violette had grown up with Josselyn's name in her head, a recording that never stopped playing in her dreams. The woman wasn't in any database she'd ever accessed. And the most surreal part was that when she finally met Josselyn, the woman didn't even know who Violette was—no idea she was talking to the general's daughter.

A shudder of grief washed over her as she found her father's lifeless body slumped in the chair behind his desk.

"No," Violette whispered. "Not this."

Josselyn lay on the floor, pale and weak. Her wavy light brown hair was streaked with blonde highlights. The locks looked dull, almost as dull as her grayed expression. Her head was in the lap of Evan Cormier.

Josselyn had given the surname of Cormier

when Violette had flown the woman onto the base. Evan's vessel had followed them. It was Violette's business to know the landing spacecrafts and who was on them—not that too many travellers wanted to visit a military compound sunk beneath sand dunes. Josselyn had been running from Evan's ship, or from someone on it. Violette didn't really care about that detail. Evan was probably trying to stop Josselyn from committing murder. Looking at the man's face now, it was obvious he loved Josselyn. His tender hands moved desperately over the woman's body, as if his willpower could save her.

For a moment, Violette thought the woman was dead and was glad for it. But the feeling was short-lived, as she took in the blue tint of Josselyn's flesh. The coloring gave away the woman's illness. Whoever had released her from her stone prison didn't finish the process. She was dying. If the syringe on the floor next to them was any indication, the general had tried to give her the cure for the stasis sickness. Every instinct inside Violette urged her to let Josselyn die.

End this now, Violette's mind whispered, *before she can get off this base. Take your revenge. Shoot her. No one will stop you. They'll give you a civilian's medal. She killed a Federation General.*

Violette's gaze found the bloody knife. It was the same slim dagger her father had used to cut her for the blood oath. She looked at her arm, to where the scar was hidden by the long sleeves of her dark shirt. That one memory kept her from leaping forward. Her promise. If it were her last act in the galaxy, she would keep her blood oath.

"Just as he said it would be," Violette stated, looking directly at Evan. Even as she saw his anguish, she couldn't bring herself to feel compassion. Not in that moment. Not for Josselyn. "I didn't want to believe him, but he has been waiting for her my whole life. He told me she would come to end him, his ghost."

"You don't understand what is happening here," Evan answered. Had the situation been different, she could have appreciated the fear in his deep brown eyes. "You can't."

"I understand that a very young girl swore a blood oath to her father." She tugged at the white cross laces running up her tight sleeve, pulling them apart to show the long scar on her forearm. "I understand that today that oath has been fulfilled. But, mostly, I understand that once Josselyn is safely off this base, and the affairs of my father are wrapped up neatly, and a new general is in place, my obligation is over. I will come for her. I will come to avenge my father, for, unlike him, I do not forgive her. When she wakes, tell her Captain Violette sends her regards."

"There is no need. She's dying. Your father killed her years ago when he imprisoned her into stone." Evan lifted Josselyn into his arms. Her limbs flopped without protest. "I recommend you find a better use of your energy. Revenge will only eat away at your soul."

"There is a chance she will survive." Violette crossed the room, going toward her father. She lifted the syringe off the floor. "He gave her the antidote. He might have killed her, but he also saved her." Then, pulling a disc key from beside her father's hand, she tossed it at Evan. He caught it, barely, as Josselyn nearly fell from his arms. "That is for her. The safe is on Quazer in the Glamour District. I'm revoking your ship's permission to stay on the base because you refused our standard inspection. Your shipmates have been unharmed and await you. I recommend you take her and go."

"Thank you," Evan said, looking as if he would say more.

"Get out of here." Violette's voice caught. She didn't want their thanks.

Evan didn't need to be told again. He carried Josselyn from the room.

Violette's anger slipped into misery. Now alone, she stumbled to her father's body. She willed him to move, to speak, to open his eyes. The alarm stopped as she knelt on the floor. Her forehead pressed into his knee as it had done when she was a little girl. The silence was more unnerving than the blaring noise. The scorched mark of a laser stained his white cotton uniform, next to the blood-ringed pierce of a knife wound. Either would have been deadly.

Death had come for her father and Violette had delivered her to his doorstep. How could he have made her do that? How could he expect her to live with herself knowing she had?

She opened her mouth to speak as she reached to touch his face. No words came out, as she thought, *I have kept my promise. I gave you my word that I would not lift a finger to stop what she chose to do. Today, my word to you is fulfilled. She made her choice and so now I make mine. Josselyn will pay for what she's done to you, as will any who try to stop me. Whatever happened to make you think this was a fair ending? You were wrong in thinking this just. I make a new promise to you. Josselyn will face justice. I promise you, father, she will pay for her sins.*

Violette lifted the knife and drew the tip along the old scar. Blood beaded up on her flesh. "I swear it by my blood, and nothing can break a blood oath." She collapsed on the floor and began to cry. "Why did you make me bring her? Why…?"

CHAPTER 4

Dev stood tense, ready for battle within the underground military base. Being trapped in a metal compound wasn't his idea of a strategic plan, but they hadn't been given a choice. Josselyn was on Rifflen seeking revenge and they had come to aid her escape. When Evan asked for help rescuing the woman he loved, Dev didn't hesitate. Once upon a time, he had been the one who needed to be saved from impossible odds. Evan's vision was the reason he was alive. Dev would do anything for his friend.

As they waited for Evan and Josselyn, Dev was well aware of the stares he received from the humanoids living beneath the sands of Rifflen. Their looks of fascination warred with terror. It was nothing new. The terror would win. When it came to him, the terror almost always won.

"Where are they, Dev? That alarm can't be a good sign." Jackson whispered under his breath. The man took a small step down the metal docking plank as if he was debating going after Evan in a premature rescue. The ship vibrated as the engines warmed. "I don't like this place. Who buries a city under the sand?"

Dev didn't answer. Jackson wouldn't expect one. The fact that they were on a Federation base didn't help. Pirates and military didn't socialize well.

Evan would contact them if he needed assistance. Besides, with Evan's psychic ability to sense the ever-changing future, he should have been able to tell them if they expected big trouble.

Dev heard a child gasp and glanced to where a hairy beast of a half-humanoid kid pointed up at him. It never made sense why people feared the red demon alien, but not the hairy ones, or the blue ones, or the slimy ones. Though, the way the Bevlons acted, it wasn't surprising. His father's people loved their evil reputation. Without giving away that he saw the kid's rude gestures, Dev turned his attention back to the metal entrance where Evan should emerge.

"Where is he?" Jackson repeated, his hands twitching.

"Hold," Dev ordered calmly. He watched as the

soldiers mingled amongst the civilians to see if they acted suspiciously. Only a few guards had responded to the alarm. The others held their place. Dev crossed his arms, silently daring them to attempt to breach the ship. None of them tried.

Inside the base, the air was stale, tainted by the gut-churning smell of roasting meats. The artificial sun lights gave a low hum. In the docking area the ceilings were high, but from what he could tell, the military base was shaped like a squashed sphere, tapering in height the closer one walked toward the outer edges. The high center point was where they entered, through a tall column that would expand out of the sands to let ships come and go. Overhead a combination of steel beams and windows did little to give the feeling of space. He wondered why they bothered with windows at all. The sand moving past the large panes made it feel like being buried alive. Below, workers aimed lasers at welded bolts, tediously reinforcing them one by one to protect the compound from sand erosion. They were quite the marksmen.

"About bloody time," Jackson swore, shaking Dev from his thoughts.

Dev followed his friend's gaze to the far side of the docks. Evan carried Josselyn, his arms strained as he rushed toward the ship. The base guards eyed

Evan as he passed. Their hostility became palpable, thickening the air.

Dev instantly moved down to the bottom of the plank to make sure no one went for a gun or tried to stop their departure. He knew Josselyn had come to Rifflen seeking revenge and had most likely found it. What he didn't understand was why the base's officials were letting them fly out of there unharmed. But then who was he to question a bit of good fortune?

"Jackson," Evan called, stumbling. Jackson rushed down the plank and across the docking area to help Evan carry Josselyn on board.

Dev's eyes swept from soldier to soldier, calculating the risk. He listened to the sound of his friends' footsteps. Suddenly, everything seemed to stop.

A woman emerged on the far side of the docks following Evan, arms crossed, green eyes hard. Curly brown hair danced around her chin as she moved. The soft locks were at odds with her fierce demeanor. The slender tailoring of her outfit, tight brown pants, and matching deep cut top, accented her tall figure. He found himself studying the curve of her hip and the long line of her legs. Her lips were pressed together in irritation, but they were full and red—the kind of lips that could command men with harsh orders or soft kisses. Dev wasn't sure which would be more effective a method, but he knew which he would prefer.

She neared the docking plank, shouldering past a few members of the crowd to stand several paces away from him. Her eyes met his. He didn't like what her look did to him. Desire surged to his surface, hotter than an exploding Bravon sun. Electric fire snapped between them. He wanted to kiss her but had a feeling she would prefer to shoot him. An entire conversation happened in that one look without words ever needing to be spoken.

"Who is that woman?" Dev asked, before he could stop himself.

Evan glanced to where he indicated. "Captain Violette. Long story, but the short version is she's not too happy with us. I'll fill everyone in once we're in orbit."

Dev didn't detect fear buried in the raw emotion swimming in Violette's gaze, not even a glimmer of it. She looked too delicate to be so tough, and yet his years of training told him not to underestimate this woman.

"Walk straight," Dev whispered gruffly, grabbing Evan's arm and practically dragging him up the plank. They needed to get off the base, but more importantly, he needed away from that woman. He didn't like the rush of emotion that filled him when he looked at her—curiosity, desire, protectiveness.

He was a warrior always ready for battle, but even he could admit when it was best to retreat. "We don't want to be stuck here waiting for the next chance to take off."

Not for the first time since it happened, Dev thought of An's curse. Evan's destiny had been realized with Josselyn when they found her imprisoned in stone on an ice tundra of a dead moon. If that was simply fate or fulfillment of a prophecy, Dev didn't know. What he did know is that he'd spent a lot of lonely nights trying to force any personal hope out of his head. And now, with one look, he was thinking she might be his element of earth as they were buried beneath the sand as their eyes met, or metal for the stretch of metal flooring that now separated them, or fire for the churning in her hot gaze and the feeling in his blood...

Or nothing. He was reaching for clues that were not there. She was nothing because men like him did not get to fall in love. His destiny lay in battle, in protecting others. He was a demon spawn after all, and who would want to love a demon?

A new alarm activated to interrupt his thoughts and break the spell of her impassioned gaze. The noise punctuated the clanking of metal against metal. The center column began to rise. Dev released Evan as they neared the top. Instantly the docking plank lifted to seal them inside the ship.

And, as he glanced through the narrowing view as the door closed, he saw the woman still stared at him with her intense eyes. She nodded once before turning her back.

Fire, Dev thought, *she is unquestionably fire.*

CHAPTER 5

THE CONQUEROR, Deep Space

"Evan and Josselyn." Rick slid into his chair at the gaming table. They were in the common area of the ship where the crew gathered to socialize with each other. "I tell you. I knew Evan and Josselyn were going to hook up from the very first moment we rescued her from her pretty little prison statue. That's why I held back with her. You know, so she didn't get lost in all my charm."

"What kind of device do you wish to hook Josselyn up to?" Dev asked, frowning. He shared a look with Jackson and Lochlann. Rick had a penchant for twenty-first century Old Earth memorabilia and sayings, and they couldn't always translate what his expressions meant.

Rick sighed dramatically. "It is all torture and

battle scars with you, isn't it, Devekin? Don't you ever think of anything else? For a hot-blooded guy, you're not very—" Rick's voice abruptly stopped as Dev stood from his chair. He held up his hands, laughing. "Easy, big fella. I'm only teasing."

Rick was right about one thing. Evan had found his true love. That accursed prophecy was at work. Dev was sure of it. How else would Evan find Josselyn so soon after Zhang An's curse?

With the newest addition of Josselyn Craven, there were eleven people on board the ship. Josselyn and Evan were in his chambers as she recovered from the last of her illness. Captain Jarek, his wife Mei, and their newborn son, Parker, passed most of their time in the captain's quarters. Other than that, everyone else spent their days in the common area.

At times, eleven felt very crowded. The isolation of deep space surrounded by the same people could become tedious, but that was the price of adventuring. It's not like Dev had anywhere else to go. Well, unless you counted the fact Dev and Jackson often escaped to the VR training facility to fight various alien species for fun—and since they'd disengaged all the safety protocols, it really was fun. If things went too wrong, there was always a medical booth on board.

Dev crossed his arms over his chest and arched a brow at Rick.

"Hook up, get together," Rick clarified, wagging his eyebrows suggestively. When no one gave him the response he was looking for, he grumbled, "Don't you have some end of days battle to prepare for, Dev? I swear if you weren't so damned ugly I'd think you and Jackson had a little something going on in the VR. Who needs to train for sixteen hours a day? It's not like we're heading off to war."

Dev didn't take offense. Whereas Dev was all about maintaining order, Rick was all about pushing the limits until they broke. Right now, Rick was bored, as often was the case when the ship was on autopilot. The man could fly his way into or out of anything. Usually, it was in and out of trouble, and he typically took everyone on the ship with him. It was hard to find mischief when surrounded by nothing but the deep black.

"What are you talking about? Dev is damned sexy." Jackson winked. He reached over to grab a hard round food chip from in front of Lucien before putting it gingerly in his mouth to try it. Then grinning, he swiped the entire bowl.

"Hey!" Lucien protested. He was half-human, half-Dere, with the strangest red-brown eyes they'd ever seen—unless they counted the red-green eyes of his older brother, Viktor. Lucien was in charge of communications, and Viktor was a mechanic who could rig anything.

"These aren't bad. Thanks." Jackson laughed, moving across the room to lounge on a low couch while he enjoyed his pilfered food.

"What *do* you guys do in the VR all day?" Rick stretched as if he'd take one of Jackson's stolen chips. Jackson pulled the bowl inches out of his reach.

"We train to save your screwboy ass," Dev answered.

"I don't need saving." Rick again tried to grab a chip and failed.

"I'll remind you of that comment next time you get kidnapped by a girl." Jackson laughed. "Again."

"Drug *queenpin*. She wasn't just a *girl*," Rick corrected. "Plus, it's fate. You can't fight fate. If I hadn't been taken, Jarek wouldn't have met Mei, Mei wouldn't have brought us to her family's palace, and, you know, you all should thank me for that prediction business. It's clear that Evan and Josselyn owe all their present happiness to me. If I didn't insult that floating b—"

"Careful, Rick," Jackson warned. "Zhang An may be dead, but she is still Mei's ancestral spirit."

"That dead ghost broad is an ancestral pain in my—" Rick tried to answer.

"Hand over the Torganian rum, space cadet," Lucien broke in. "It's clear you're hallucinating grandeur again."

"Yeah, you must be crazy if you think the guys are going to thank you for that little stunt you pulled," Viktor added.

"Still too soon to joke about the curse?" Rick inquired, giving a playful smile. Everyone who knew Rick recognized that he felt sorry about what had happened but would never allow himself to admit it. The man hid his emotions behind jokes.

The curse.

Violette. Her name was Violette. Josselyn's sister. The dead general's daughter. Angry, beautiful Violette.

Dev's stomach tightened at the reminder of the curse, but he didn't let his emotions show. There wasn't an hour that had passed that he didn't think about Zhang An's words since seeing Violette on the docks. It wasn't just that she was one of the most beautiful creatures he'd ever beheld; it was the pain in her eyes. Deep, soulful green eyes.

"You will find your love hidden within the mystery of the five elements. If you do not recognize it, you will lose it and be forever alone."

He found himself wondering not for the first time which element Violette might be.

Sand-covered base? Was she earth?

Fire? Was he fire? Were her eyes fire?

Metal? The military base was metal.

Water? He had no idea. Humans were a water-based species, but that hardly seemed like a mystical sign.

Wood? He glanced down at his lap and shifted his hips uncomfortably. Rick had a crude term for, well...

Dev grimaced. Why was he doing this to himself? He didn't need a spirit to tell him he'd be forever alone. He could predict that for himself every time he looked in the mirror. Demon. Devil. Damned. He'd been called it all. No sane human woman would want that by her side unless it were to be her bodyguard.

Captain Violette.

He was foolish to even allow himself to think of her. After they cleared Rifflen's skies and were on their way into deep space, Evan had informed them that Josselyn stabbed the general, and then Evan shot the man in an effort to cover up the crime. It didn't work. Violette suspected the truth.

"Rick, I would have liked to see you get blasted by a ghost lady." Viktor laughed, pulling Dev from his thoughts. "I can't believe you tried to lure a dead woman into your bed."

"Now that would have been funny," Lucien agreed.

"Easy for you two to laugh about. This rock-etboy didn't curse you," Lochlann drawled.

"As the acting security officer on this ship, I give

you permission to beat Rick's ass again," Jackson said, directing his gaze at Lochlann.

"Well, if you do that, I won't tell you where the ship is heading," Rick feigned nonchalance. "Captain just gave me our new coordinates."

"Back to the frozen tundra of Florencia's Fifth Moon?" Lucien guessed. "To collect our treasure?"

"To check if there are any more sexy women waiting to be thawed from prison like Josselyn?" Viktor inquired. Before they arrived on the Fifth Moon to rescue her, Josselyn had been left in an abandoned prison, frozen in stone for over a hundred years on a forgotten corner of deep space.

Maybe Josselyn was earth. She'd been held in a stone-like state. Yet the planet was covered in ice, so she could be water.

The vagueness of the curse was going to drive Dev into madness.

"Wrong. Received *new* coordinates. Typed them in about an hour ago." Rick grinned. "With orders to fly erratically to avoid a certain she-captain's pursuit before we get where we're going."

At that Dev involuntarily stiffened. "Pursuit?"

"Easy, Barbecue Boy, stand down, no one's trying to burn you alive just yet," Rick admonished. "We're not flying into battle. It's only that Violette girl."

"Evan told me she's sworn revenge on Josselyn for killing the general," Lucien said.

"Vengeful Violette," Rick stated, grinning at the nickname he'd just made up for her. "Vengeful Violette is a vivacious villain, very vindictive—"

"Someone shoot Ricochet Rick over there," Lochlann interrupted. The men laughed.

"Seriously, though, have you stopped to think about this?" Rick turned contemplative as if he was focusing. "Violette is Josselyn's half-sister. They share a mother, Lady Craven. Josselyn was born over a hundred years ago on a Florencian moon and then imprisoned in stone after everyone, excluding her mother, was massacred with the help of the general. Violette was born later to the general and Lady Craven, who did not know the kind of bastard her second husband truly was. When Josselyn was freed from prison, her preserved body *looks* roughly the same age as her sister." Rick paused expectantly.

Such events made it highly unlikely Dev would ever see Violette on friendly terms. He had a loyalty to his family, and Violette had sworn to avenge her father. That didn't stop the desire from boiling his blood. Moreover, he was sure the challenge made him want her more.

When no one seemed to get his point, Rick continued, "Guys, don't you see what this means?

Evan's woman is like over a hundred years old. He's doing a—"

"Ach," Lochlann waved his hand in dismissal as Rick began to chuckle.

"You're one to talk," Lucien added. "You tried to proposition an elderly spirit woman."

"That Violette isn't bad looking, but a little hard for my tastes," Rick stated. "She's the kind that would take a lot of work. Only liquor should be hard. I prefer my women soft."

"Don't you mean easy?" Lochlann drawled.

"I think he meant on discount," Jackson teased.

"Who are you kidding, Rick?" Lucien chuckled. "You'll take any female that'll have you."

"Jealousy is not pretty on you three," Rick retorted. Then laughing, he said, "Yeah, you're right, though. Difficult to pass up a good pleasure droid that's on discount."

Dev didn't speak. He wasn't much of a talker anyway. In some ways, he envied Rick's ability to converse with whoever happened to be within earshot. *Not* that he would ever tell the irritating man as much. The last thing Rick's ego needed was a boost.

Dev's silence didn't stem from a sense of superiority of those around him, nor did it come from disinterest or stupidity. It just wasn't in his nature to participate. He watched, listened, protected, studied. Perhaps it was a trademark of his youth, from a time when it was better to be on guard and not draw attention to himself, never knowing when his father's people were going to have a go at him—the half-beast weakling.

"You tell me where we're going," Lucien said, walking across the commons to reach behind a chair. He pulled out a bottle of whiskey, "and I'll let you see the new pleasure droid commercials I caught on the airwaves last night. They were the encoded ones, from the Zenni District."

Rick instantly pushed up from his chair and answered, "Quazer. Glamour District. That general guy that Josselyn killed left her a security box there and we're going to check it out with her. Captain Violette is following us. We're hoping to shake her." He reached for the bottle of whiskey and hooked Lucien's arm. "Did they really come from the Zenni District? They show *every* function on those advertisements."

"Each one lasts twenty-six minutes—*per unit!*" Lucien answered. The two men disappeared through the door, still talking about the rogue airwaves.

"Well," Lochlann said, faking indifference. "Couldn't hurt to have a peek at the new models." As Lochlann took a step for the door, Viktor shot to his feet. Both men raced after Lucien. Lochlann beat the smaller man by a few paces. Dev heard them running down the hall, pushing into each other as they tried to catch up.

When they were alone, Jackson said, "Ignore Rick. He doesn't mean anything by what he says. We both know that fly boy is more damaged than any of us."

Dev frowned. "I wasn't thinking about Rick."

"Oh," Jackson answered, surprised. "I saw your eyes narrow. You appeared upset." After countless hours training together, Jackson could read him pretty well.

"I am going to run space battle simulations in the VR." Dev stood and moved to go. Captain Violette wouldn't leave his thoughts. The obsession was strange. He'd only seen her that one time, standing in the distance, staring at him. He'd never heard her voice, never touched her, never smelled her, but those eyes of hers, tormented and raw with emotion, contrasting the rigid pride in her slender body. She was strength and beauty and…

What was he doing? Dev looked at his hands, to the subtle darker red markings on his flesh. They only showed at certain times and were so faint most people didn't notice them. Violette was a human woman. She was starlight and moonshine. He looked like something from one of those Old Earth transmission waves Lucien captured and saved for them—a beast, an evil possessor, the thing of nightmares humans were always trying to kill. Violette represented everything he could ever want and yet could never have. All she could ever be to a man like him was a name, an idea…a nemesis after his family.

"I'll join you," Jackson said. "I could go a few rounds with a Torg before bed."

"No, not this time. I need to practice my solo fight. Why don't you join the others?" Dev didn't break stride as he left.

CHAPTER 6

Glamour District, Quazer

Vengeance. Even the word left Violette feeling dead inside. It wasn't like she *wanted* to kill the woman. She had to. Honor was the only piece of her family she had left.

Violette knew Josselyn would appear in the Glamour District eventually. How could the woman resist seeing what inheritance the general had left her? It's the whole reason Violette had given over the security disc to Evan. It wasn't like she cared if the woman had a new start to a new life.

No. Violette wanted to be sure she could track Josselyn down. The woman killed her father. That is all Violette needed to know. The details of why didn't matter.

The general had forced Violette to step aside

and let Josselyn do whatever she wanted. He had even gone so far as to order Violette to help the woman onto the base. Now, with both parents dead and a new general on Rifflen, she had nothing beyond her ship, her crew, her name, and family honor.

Unfortunately for her, her ship was a yellow chunk of space scrap called *Racing Banana*. The sharp angles of its front nose turned upward at the end. Dark red stripes added an elongated effect to the shape as they stood out from the almost too bright color of the ship's yellow body. Ok, calling it "junk" was a little harsh. It wasn't a pile of rust, nor was it a luxury ship. It shook a little too hard when leaving a planet's atmosphere and it used way too much fuel. She would never say as much to her pilot, Jo. He believed his "lady" was the fastest piece of spacecraft beauty ever invented. Violette thought better than to get into the middle of that strange alien-machine relationship.

Sure, there was her inheritance—space credits to keep her living comfortably if she was smart, a list of contacts if she ever needed anything, and her father's legacy. But space credits and a list of names wasn't the same as family.

As for her crew, they were nonconformists, all of them, and the product of her alientarian father's influence. Jo was Slit'therne, part of a snake-like race of aliens found in remote, swampy locations. He had a human-shaped upper body, except that green-yellow scales replaced flesh and webbed hands. He slithered when he moved, propelling himself along with a tail appendage replacing what would have been legs.

Their mechanic, Gil, was Angelion, a race reminiscent of Old Earth culture's angels, minus the benevolence. The blue-white of his feathered wings rested along his backside, nearly touching the floor. Besides a ridge on his chest, his front side looked to be human. Violette didn't know much about Old Earth's angel race, but she knew Gil was far from what she would consider holy.

Isaac, their Corge crewman, came in handy for just about anything they needed him to do. He lacked the hesitance—and the conscience—that plagued most people. A large black horn protruded from the center of his blue forehead. It had a crack along the tip. Corge men emitted a sweet smell that took some getting used to. Violette often supposed the reason for his aloofness was because he couldn't feel pain, or pleasure, at least in the physical sense.

The last crewman was a Thinean they called Ghost. He was a thin, pale man who rarely left the ship, and seldom showed himself to those on board. It was easy to forget he was there. For all she knew he slept in some crack in her hull.

"*Sacre*," Violette swore as she stared at the viewing screen. "What is taking them so long to land?"

"Patience, Captain," Isaac answered, his tone reasonable. "No reason to rush your revenge."

Isaac had suggested they let Josselyn go so they could spend the next five years chasing her around the galaxy for fun. Though Violette liked a good pursuit as much as any other space adventurer, she wasn't a cruel person by nature. She didn't want to draw out her vengeance. She wanted it over with.

"Do you think we'll have a problem with her crew?" Gil asked, coming inside the cockpit. "The man you described sounds Bevlon, at least in part. They're not to be trusted. The fact that they carry one on board is not a good sign."

Violette stiffened. Bevlons were the ancient enemies of the Angelion. She didn't judge so harshly, but then her ancestors hadn't spent a near eternity locked in battle with the Bevlon race. Yet, and she would never admit it to Gil, she couldn't stop thinking about the man. At first glance, he'd appeared all red, but when she stared at him, she saw he had thin darker lines scrolling his flesh. His black eyes had caused a small chill inside her soul— and not at all in a bad way. The more she thought about him, the more she found herself oddly attracted to him. The fact that he was Bevlon, or part Bevlon, didn't bother her. Inter-alien relationships weren't frowned upon in deep space ports—at least not by anyone she cared to listen to.

There was an expression in the man's eyes that Violette knew well. She felt the hollow echo of it in her soul. It was loneliness and sadness and longing, but it was also the hope that those things would not last forever, and the fear that they would. The man haunted her. Possibly, it was the idea of him that haunted her.

Or, maybe, it was because she'd been without a lover for a very long time and the Bevlon was the first man she'd felt any kind of attraction for.

Sacre.

What was she thinking? He was a member of the crew who saved Josselyn. It was just like her to choose someone to fantasize over that she could never have.

"*Sacre*," she cursed again. Then realizing her men were staring at her, she squared her shoulders. "Make port with the secure codes so no one will know we're here. They have to suspect we might show, and I don't want them getting a heads up. I know the securities building she's going to. We'll catch up with them there. And remember. No one touches Josselyn. She's mine."

The crewmen nodded. Gil made a small sound of approval. Isaac grinned.

"Never trust anyone who travels with a Bevlon," Gil warned. "Watch your back. They're treacherous beasts."

Violette didn't answer.

Jo activated a com-link with the Docking Master and began the lengthy process of setting up a secure military code landing. Having Federation ties did have its perks.

"Take your revenge, but if we run into trouble, the Bevlon is mine." Gil smiled. His wings lifted, and he hovered over the floor. Then, leaning back, he dove into the air, gliding through the smaller cockpit door. For such large wings, he really was an agile flyer.

"This is not your fault," Isaac stated when Gil was gone.

Violette didn't keep secrets from Isaac. They'd known each other for too long. "I brought her to the base. I led her right to my father."

"You were under orders. If you didn't fetch her, the general would have sent someone else." Isaac grabbed her wrist and lifted her arm. He ran his finger over the long scar through the clothing. "You did what you had to."

"I should have known she'd kill him." Violette looked at her arm before tugging it away. "My oath is finished. I never promised not to take revenge. I only promised not to interfere with what she planned." She still hated her father for forcing the blood oath on her. "I don't care what my father said. Whatever wrong my father thought to have dealt her, it was nothing to justify the killing of a great man."

"There are perhaps things we don't know," Isaac reasoned.

"Since when do you try to be rational?" Violette quipped in irritation. The last thing she wanted was doubt, in herself or in her crew. "If you don't wish to come with me, you can stay behind. I—"

"Oh, I'll come, and I'll fight whoever you put in front of me just for the sport of it," Isaac interrupted. "I have no fear of battles. What I do fear is what that battle will do to you if you do not first learn the story. When it is over, you will begin to wonder. That wonder will turn to doubt. Doubt to self-doubt to insecurity and second-guessing. You will be useless as a captain, and I have no desire to acquire work on a new ship. The story won't change the fact you need to deal with the woman, but it will keep your mind forward. I find humans need that sort of reasoning."

"Your concern is overwhelming," she drawled.

Isaac made an indifferent gesture. "How humanoids have evolved to be the most populated races, I will never understand."

"It's called breeding," Violette answered.

"Remind me and I'll explain the concept sometime."

"You're not my type." Isaac gave a small glance toward the door. It was no secret to her that Isaac had a thing for winged men. Gil did not return the sentiment.

"Glad to hear it. This day is already starting on a high note." Violette turned her attention to Jo as he hung up the com-link to the docks.

"We're all set. Should be a smooth set down. Quazer has luxury atmospheric generators."

"As soon as we land, inquire about *The Conqueror*. Find out where she's docked." Violette turned to leave. "Arm up. With those Federation codes, no one will check us. We're going in with weapons."

"I do enjoy a good hunt," Isaac said.

THE WHITE STREETS SHIMMERED IN THE BRIGHT sunlight as a tropical breeze filtered through the Glamour District. Smooth stone arches with crystal insets lined the sidewalks, creating colorful streaks of light on the ground. As a planet entirely dedicated to luxury and the wealthy, Quazer had docking fees, security fees and a long list of other charges designed to ensure only those who could afford to be there actually landed. Violette paid for none of those with her Federation codes. The district was filled with nobles, the rich and famous from around the galaxy. Their demeanor and actions spoke of money and power, and enough snobbery that they tended to ignore her.

"Where's Gil?" Violette asked.

They had tracked Josselyn and Evan to the securities building where she'd open whatever the general had left behind for her. The building glistened like all the other shops. Laser protection bars striped the windows and encrusted silver lined the intricately carved signs. It wouldn't be wise to take their weapons in, so Violette decided to wait. There was only one public exit, and she was staring straight at it.

"Jo found the ship," Isaac answered, keeping behind her. "Gil went to place a tracking beacon on it, just in case."

She nodded. "Good."

Violette's eyes narrowed as she saw her target. Josselyn wore a lightweight pink two-piece dress. The skirt moved with the breeze, but the tight bodice molded to her, forming a cocoon of hard material. The woman looked deceptively normal, but there she was, the murderer who killed a great man.

Evan was with her. That undoubtedly meant the others were close. She glanced over the crowd but didn't see the Bevlon. It was probably for the best. The last time she'd locked eyes with him she'd gone brain numb.

Violette's stomach clenched, and her heartbeat quickened as she approached Josselyn.

"Vengeance," she whispered. It was as if that one word drew Josselyn's eyes to her though there was no way the woman heard what she said. "We follow her."

To Violette's surprise, Josselyn didn't run. Instead, she calmly moved forward, clutching a black bag to her chest. Unbidden, Violette's gaze moved to it, curious as to what her father would have left for the woman. A wave of grief hit her, but she swallowed it down. She glanced around the busy street only to catch a glimpse of Isaac working his way through the crowd to keep an eye on the situation.

"You're braver than I thought," Violette said when the woman was close enough to hear her. Her breathing deepened. Oh, how she wanted to scream, to hit. She kept calm. "Or more stupid."

"I won't speak ill of your father to you, but the man you knew is not the Jack I did." Josselyn stopped walking, keeping distance between them. Evan stayed protectively close to her.

"I think I knew him much better than you." Violette set her jaw, her eyes narrowing. Inside she trembled with rage and grief, but beneath that stirred a tiny thread of curiosity. Isaac was right. Part of her wanted to know why, *needed* to know the truth. That thread grew, twisting its way into her psyche. It kept her from reaching beneath the hem of her shirt and drawing her weapon.

"Before your mother—" Josselyn began.

"My mother died when I was born." How dare this woman speak of her mother?

"Before she married Jack..." Josselyn didn't move as she hesitated. "She was my mother."

A half-sister? Violette snorted in disbelief. "Is that what this is? Mommy left you and so you sought revenge on the man who won her heart?"

Josselyn didn't rise to the bait. Violette wished she would. She wanted any excuse to justify pulling her gun to scare the woman. *Sacre*! She'd even take a good old-fashioned fistfight.

So, was that why her father felt guilty? He fell in love with another man's wife? So what? Marriages ended every day.

Josselyn reached into the black bag and pulled out a holo-box. "You *are* my sister and I don't wish you any harm. Long ago, when your father was a young man, he knew me and was protected by my father, Lord Craven. We grew up together in my castle home on Florencia's Fifth Moon. Jack betrayed us and was part of the invasion that took our homes, our lives and imprisoned me in stone. I'm sure your father was a changed man, but he knew he had to pay for his past sins. Because of him, thousands of our people died, your mother's people."

"My father was a humanitarian. Because of him millions lived," Violette said. "My mother was a lady, a fine lady he'd saved. I did not interfere before because I promised him I wouldn't, but that promise is fulfilled, and I will not stop until you pay for what you have done."

"I didn't expect you to believe me, but before you ruin your life chasing revenge and trying to get to me, watch this." Josselyn tossed the holo-box at her. "Perhaps your father's words will convince you to find a better path."

Violette caught the holo-box but didn't look at it as Josselyn backed away from her. Evan's hand glided onto the woman's arm, and he escorted her into the crowd. Violette slipped behind a group of women to disappear from sight while keeping an eye on her. Josselyn glanced back but didn't see her.

"We'll follow her," Isaac said, joining her side. "We'll kill them both away from the security cameras and be done with this. Afterward, I'll buy you a drink."

"No," Violette answered, gripping the holo-box tight. She didn't want to admit that she'd hesitated.

Josselyn had spoken, and Violette had been unable to pull her gun on her. "We're leaving."

"What?" Isaac stiffened. "Have you lost your nerve? Did the two humans make friends?"

"Stow it," she ordered. Violette kept her tone hard to hide the doubt she was feeling. "You were right. She doesn't deserve a quick death. I'll hunt her instead."

Isaac nodded in approval. "Ah, that's the right spirit." He directed his stare after Josselyn and Evan. "We'll take everything she loves first and then you will have your final revenge. This is the better plan."

Violette couldn't answer. She knew what duty called her to do, and yet she wasn't a killer. When Isaac wouldn't stop studying her expression, she nodded. "Let's find the others."

CHAPTER 7

Dev didn't like this. Not at all.

The Glamour District welcomed all kinds of species, but he didn't feel comfortable traveling within the rich crowd. His crewmen were trying to blend and all his appearance tended to do was the opposite. It always amazed him how many intelligent, educated people still believed demons and devils looked like Bevlons. In Dev's experiences, demons were much more ordinary and deceptively normal.

No, that was just an excuse he told the captain. He was lying to himself. The real reason he stayed on the ship was because he was afraid of seeing Violette again. She was inside his head. When he closed his eyes, he saw her face. The idea of her was all he could think about—those emotion-filled eyes, those parted lips, that proud stance. He didn't want to face her in a fight. He didn't want to have to choose between his family and an idea. His dreams were filled with her, of moments and touches that could never be. Dev didn't want those dreams to end, even as they tortured him. Reality had a way of crushing dreams.

After stopping to check on Parker to make sure the electronic caretaker was in working order, and that the baby's room security codes were locked in, he made his way back toward his private quarters. Like most rooms on the ship his was small, metal and equipped with all the necessities. The bed unit was attached to the wall, and he was thankful the mattress was spacious enough to hold his larger size. Dev didn't bother to decorate the walls, and he kept his belongings in an old cargo box under his bed.

Dev made a move to lie down when suddenly the ship's security alarm beeped in warning. Without hesitation, he ran out the door toward the cockpit. He thought of Parker and almost turned back around but knew that the security codes were entered correctly since he'd done them himself. The baby would be safe. Jarek had pre-programmed the caretaker unit with every contingency plan imaginable, including a pod function that would transport the child across the stars to one of his parents' home planets should anything happen to the ship.

Reaching the cockpit, Dev glanced at the security monitor. The outside hull showed on the viewing screen. Every muscle tensed, ready for battle. Someone leaned close to the underbelly of the vessel. Thankfully, they were not trying to breach the entry hatch. Dev took the controls and launched a tiny camera orb to get a better view. The figure's body quivered beneath a long coat.

Dev grimaced. "Blasted drunks. Find somewhere else to lose your liquor." Recalling the camera to the ship, he automatically felt for the gun at his side before going to the hatch to scare the man away. The last thing they wanted was vomit on the side of the vessel. Plus, as mundane as it was, frightening a drunk gave him something to do. Hitting the button to open the hatch, he didn't wait for the deck to lower all the way before he started walking down the metal plank. He grabbed onto a metal protrusion and leaned over.

"Out of here, rocket boy," he growled in his meanest tone. His naturally low voice made it easy to strike fear into others. "Foul up your own ship!"

When he looked to where the man had been leaning, he frowned. The drunk was gone, but there was something not right about the scene. It was too clean. Dev didn't stop to question his initial instinct as he turned to run back into the ship. His hand lifted to the security scanner on the hatch. As he pressed his hand flat, a sharp pain radiated from his stomach, and then another. The feeling of electrical current ran through him. His vision blurred as the plank beneath his feet moved. He swayed violently. Someone had shot him with electric darts. They seared his clothing and flesh, burning hotter with each passing second.

Dev's knees trembled, but he kept his footing long enough to hear the ship's security system beep as it armed itself to protect the child. The sound was the last he heard as his body tumbled backward. His head struck metal, and he rolled off the rising plank into darkness.

CHAPTER 8

VIOLETTE STARED at the holographic image of her father in a shiny white suit. He looked a lot younger than she remembered him being though this particular recording was as familiar a childhood memory as any. Tapping her finger on the holo-box, she drew her hand back. She'd played it nearly twenty times in the last hour, yet found herself listening again to the well-known voice. She missed her father, missed seeing him and hearing him. Nevertheless, the words were as unbelievable to her now as they were when she was eight.

"Josselyn, I'm glad you are well." Jack's image said. Violette ran her finger over her scar as the recording played. "It's what I've hoped for these last, long years. By this time and because you are still alive after the term of your imprisonment has ended, we have probably spoken. Knowing the temperament of your family, we have not spoken kindly. So much has happened and changed since that day long ago, and I have to force myself to remember that you don't know the good I've tried to do. All you know is my sins. I cannot take back that which was done, but I can give you a new life. With these papers, you will never have to explain your age or your past. As my daughter, a general's daughter, you will have the freedom to pass by Federation ports unhampered. I cannot leave the life I have chosen. The Federation has granted me the home, which I so longed to be a part of in those years you knew me, as a reward for my services. I know it is not the land it once was, but all it is, I give to you."

Her father continued on to explain modern space life as if talking to…well, to a woman who'd missed the last hundred years of technology. He walked through how to use space credits and identification papers. He gave Josselyn directions to a mostly automated personal vessel with navigational guides to assist her in flying it. On the ship, the woman would find clothing and a machine to download knowledge into her brain to help her function in the new time. The general had thought of everything, even supplied a list of possible new home worlds and directions to them, should she decide to relocate. Violette listened to all of it with a stone in her stomach, lump in her throat, and a heart that ached so badly she wanted to cut it out of her chest.

"If, by some miracle, you can forgive me, I would welcome you back into the family," Jack continued. "Though it remains my greatest wish, I fear you will never take me up on this offer. What you might not have discovered is that your mother was my wife. I will not presume to call myself your father-by-marriage though legally speaking I am just that, which is why the papers I give you call you my daughter. Do not toss those papers aside. You will not be able to survive in the current world without them. I want you to know that I took care of Lady Craven, but she was never the same after our world was destroyed. I did not tell her about your fate. I did not want to give her false hope."

A tear slipped over Violette's cheek.

"From our union, you have a sister. We named her Violette after the moonflower petals your mother dearly loved. Our Violette is strong willed and smart. She reminds me of you as a child, rebellious to a fault, but with a heart bigger than the entire universe. Lady Craven did not survive the birthing. Please, for your mother, do not seek revenge against your sister for my crimes. She is your blood. I sometimes long for what we could have been to each other, should life have been less cruel. I don't blame you for I see the impossibility of us now, but you must know that I loved you then, as part of me continues to love you even now. I would have proudly been your husband, but you know that. You know all of that. I sometimes forget how fresh the events must be to you. There was so much death between us. That said, if there is to be another death, or more to the point if I am dead, I hope it was in atonement of my sins and that you will be able to forgive me now. I am truly sorry, Josselyn. All I ever wanted was to be a part of what you had. I never meant to destroy that which I loved so dearly." Jack sighed, and she could see the pain on his face. He nodded once before the holo-box turned off.

Was it an apology or a love letter or a justification of some past tragedy? Was Josselyn a daughter or fiancée? Though it filled in a great piece of the puzzle, it only caused more questions to arise. What had happened? And how did this information change the fact that Josselyn had killed a great man, her father? If Josselyn was imprisoned that had to mean the woman had done something wrong. Violette knew the general. He would never harm an innocent person. Never.

Violette crossed her arms over her chest and sat back. Her shoulders hit the metal wall of her sparsely decorated captain's quarters. In reality, the only thing separating her room from the rest of the crews' was that she was in it. Otherwise, they were identical.

Her father's voice echoed through her. Sister?

What kind of strange family history lesson was this? The general wanted to marry Josselyn a hundred years ago. Instead, there was a betrayal, and he married the mother—Josselyn's mother, *Violette's* mother. Josselyn was frozen in a Federation prison for some crime related to the treachery, thawed, came back to kill the old man who knew her in their youth, and was now walking around looking and acting the same age as Violette with a birthday technically in the prior century.

Just thinking about it made her head hurt.

This bit of news did put a small crimp in her plans. As far as Violette knew, Josselyn was her only living relative—unless of course her father had more secrets floating around the universe. The general would demand that she respected the shared blood.

"Well, he's not here, is he?" Violette said to the empty room. She slammed her fist back into the wall, making a satisfying bang against the metal.

Three seconds later an answering bang vibrated back. She felt more than heard it. Her mind came to full alert. The vibrations sounded again, louder this time. They became a steady beating against the metal of her ship. She knew every noise *Racing Banana* made. This was not one of them.

Forgetting her personal concerns as she went to investigate, Violette ran her hand along the corridor, feeling for the vibrations. They grew stronger toward the back of the ship. She imagined the rest of the crew to be sleeping—even the pilot. On board a vessel it was hard to keep track of day and night since they were in deep space, so they kept the ship's lights on a dim timer. It helped regulate sleep patterns and kept the crew from going crazy.

The noise was coming from the cargo hold. Violette grimaced in annoyance. "Blast it all, Isaac, if you smuggled another unsanctioned creature onto this ship again, I'll have your Corge ass!"

The small room was crammed full of metal boxes and rubber-coated crates. There was barely enough room to maneuver down the narrow aisle between the stacked cargo. Seeing movement, she stiffened.

"*Sacre*, Ghost, you startled me. Is that you making all that noise? What's going on?" Violette took a deep breath, only to have the renewed banging pull her attention.

Ghost pointed at a large crate in the back and then moved to disappear into a narrow opening between two boxes. Violette glanced after him as she passed. She'd barely be able to get her hand into the tiny space.

"Thanks for the assistance," she yelled sarcastically after him. The pounding became louder. She stiffened, apprehensive of what she faced. There was no telling what manner of creature her crewmen had smuggled on. Gentling her voice, she stepped lightly. "Easy there." The banging stopped. "There you go. What's in there making all that noise? Huh?" She fingered the latch but then drew her hand back. Without a shipping label or any idea of what she'd be unleashing, she couldn't just blindly open the box—no matter how curious she was to see inside. Moving to peer into a dark breathing hole, she whispered, "I just need to find out what you are before I let you free."

She saw movement and leaned closer.

"I am Salebinaben Johobik en Dehauberkelsain en Thoraxian en Yyrtolzx Devekin, and you will release me immediately," a gruff male voice answered.

The last thing Violette expected was to get an actual answer. A man? Someone on her crew abducted a man?

"Ah, I, ah," she stammered, trying to reason

what was happening on her vessel. Some captain she was. Apparently, they were in the kidnapping business, and she didn't even know it. "What are you doing on this ship? Are you a stowaway?" She couldn't help the hopeful note to her voice. Sure, that was it. A person sneaked on and accidentally latched themselves inside a crate…with a manual iron lock on the outside of the box…in the back cargo hold of a secured ship…on a special dock reserved for Federation…oh, blasted nova. This was bad.

"Let me out," he demanded. The man clearly was used to being obeyed. The tone of his voice filled her with a strange mix of pleasure and aggravation.

She ignored the command. "What are you doing on my ship?"

"You tell me," he snapped. "It's not like I put myself in a shipping container."

"Shouldn't you try to at least sweet talk your way out of that box? You're in no position to make demands." She leaned over, trying to see him. All she could detect was blackness.

His answer was a grave, humorless laugh.

"How did you come to be on this ship?" she enunciated each word.

He hit the inside of the box, making her jump back a little. Her heart pounded. Calmer than before, he said, "Send me your captain. I want to talk to whoever is in charge. You obviously have no authority here."

"*I* am the captain," Violette answered, straightening. "I have complete authority here."

"Do you?" he mocked. "Then how is it *I* am on your ship, and *you* have no idea why or how I've come to be here. Clearly, you do not have complete authority over this vessel because one of your crew is going about abducting people on your watch without your knowledge. You may have the honorary title of captain, but you are a figurehead and not in charge. Send me whoever has the authority to make decisions."

"Honorary?" she gasped. No one ever dared to talk to her like that. Even when she was little, the soldiers had shown her the respect due both her family name and her father's position within the Federation Military.

"What's wrong, Spacecake, did I hurt your feelings?"

"Spacecake?" she repeated, her tone growing hard in her anger. "Listen here my caged semikin, you are in no position to throw around insults. At my word you'll be left in that box to decompose!"

"So you kill innocent people to prove your rank? With such ethics, I must be on a Federation ship."

He paused before laughing. "Did you just call me a semikin?"

"You are—"

His laughter grew louder.

"You—" she tried again.

"Semikin," he repeated, louder. He didn't sound so threatening when he laughed.

Unsure why she made the decision, she said, "Give me a moment. I'm going to get you out of there and then we'll figure out how you came to be delivered to my ship by mistake." The smart thing would have been to question her crew. "We don't take prisoners, and you hardly seem like cargo."

"Hardly," he repeated dryly.

"I don't suppose it will be necessary to threaten you with what will happen to you should you try anything. We're out in deep space. I have no problem catapulting you into oblivion."

"Understood."

"What manner of creature are you?" Violette hesitated. Some aliens considered what she'd just asked a complete violation of etiquette.

"Humanoid," he answered curtly. She believed him. He sounded humanoid and spoke the well-known Old Star language.

Why was she hesitating? She was the captain. She had good instincts. This was her ship. She could defend herself if needed. Reaching between two boxes to where a laser was kept hidden, she aimed it at the latch.

"Don't move," Violette ordered before shooting a short blast. The lock sizzled and popped. A second later the lid burst open, and a giant red figure appeared before her. He lunged before her eyes could focus. On instinct, she jumped back and discharged a warning shot. The man growled. Violette's hip hit the edge of a container, tripping her. She fell to the floor. The hard grated texture of the ship's walkway bit into her skin as she slid a few inches. It was enough to rub the flesh of her side raw.

"Don't move." This time the order was given to her.

She blinked back the pain as she lifted her weapon. Something struck her wrist, knocking the gun from her hand. Before she knew what was happening, a large body pinned hers to the ground. Fingers gripped her wrist, pushing it down tight to the grate. She softly moaned as thighs pinned her sore hip. It wasn't the pain so much as the close contact. It took her a moment for her eyes to focus on the man who held her.

Black eyes pierced her with their intensity. She shivered. "You."

For an instant, she couldn't draw breath.

He stared down at her. "You."

"I remember you. You're from Josselyn's ship. The Bevlon security officer." As she said the words, it didn't take long for her to figure out what had probably happened. Gil.

"Devekin," he supplied. "Dev."

Violette rocked her body, trying to free herself. The solid wall of muscle pinning her down didn't budge. If anything, the movement only pressed him closer, making her all too aware of how intimately they touched.

A tiny ripple of pleasure moved through her. His strength excited her, as did his hard body and piercingly dark eyes. The fact that darker lines threaded the red hue of his flesh, and the very look of him proved to be something wickedly sinful, did not bother her. She found it exciting. *Sacre!* She found it downright sexy. Violette's breathing deepened. She bucked her hips again, but the motion lacked the angry bid for freedom that it had carried before.

"Captain Violette," Dev stated. "I suspected your crew, but you gain nothing by capturing me. My people will not trade me for your sister."

Thinking of Josselyn caused her to stiffen. "Get off me."

He didn't move.

"Get. Off. Me," she ordered again.

"You're not in a position to give me orders." He studied her carefully.

"You're in the middle of deep space on my ship. You're not really in a position to not take my orders," she answered.

The battle of wills between them was palpable, and she wasn't sure who would come out the victor.

CHAPTER 9

DEV PUSHED TO HIS FEET, letting go of the woman he held prisoner against the floor. He'd trapped her on instinct, only seeing who she was once he had her pinned beneath him. Violette.

Beautiful Violette.

The impression of her toned flesh stung his hands and legs, arousing the deep passions he'd worked so hard to suppress. He never thought he'd touch her, not like this. His skin tingled until it ached. In the darkest hours, he'd imagined this woman, convincing himself that the only time he would see her was in battle should she try to harm Josselyn.

The rush of his nocturnal fantasies filled him, and he wished with all his might that this was a dream. If it were, she'd kiss him soon, and they would have angry, hard, sweaty sex right there on the floor. His cock ached at the very notion. All it would take was one gesture on her part to show she was willing, and he'd have her naked and impaled before she could blink.

Her voice matched her eyes—filled with passion and determination. He craved to hear her whisper his name with those sweet lips. If he'd been hopeless before, he was completely captured by her spell now. There was no explaining it. She pulled him to her like a magnet. It took everything in him to resist.

As he stood, he wanted to stretch his cramped muscles. The cargo container had not been the most comfortable of cages, but he'd been locked inside worse. While confined in the dark, the old fear had threatened him. His type wasn't exactly safe from religious zealots, and their way of ridding the world of his kind of "evil" usually involved a rather painful and public execution.

Seeing Violette calmed that panic. This foe he could handle. She was one woman…one very exquisite, delicate, starbeam of a woman.

Blast it all!

Maybe he couldn't handle her.

Oh, please let her kiss him. It wasn't in him to take an unwilling woman but a single sign, that's all his body needed.

Suddenly, she began to chuckle as she pushed

herself up from the floor. He wasn't expecting the sound, and it took him off guard. Dev wasn't sure if he should be offended, so he held perfectly still. Her laughter grew. When he could take it no longer, he asked, "What?"

"I was just thinking," she said, calming herself, "no one would ever mistake a great beast of a man like you for a little semikin."

Dev didn't share in her humor. He saw the irony, but couldn't force himself to smile. At his lack of participation, she sobered. He was sorry to see the merriment fade from her eyes but did nothing to bring it back.

Already he calculated a way to overtake the vessel. Seeing the captain, he could well deduce he was on *Racing Banana*. The ship was small. He could man it solo until he was rescued. Now, all he would have to do is determine if the layout matched what he'd studied in the VR, subdue the crew, and fly himself to a safe port if *The Conqueror* wasn't close enough to answer his distress call. It should be simple enough.

"I see we are beyond pretending my being brought here was an accident," he stated. Her lack of answer was answer aplenty. "I thought as much. What's the plan? Ransom? Trade? Torture for information?" He arched a brow. "Slavery?"

"All valid reasons to have someone taken," she agreed. "But I didn't order you—"

The door slid open behind her, drawing their attention around to the front of the cargo hold.

Dev's eyes narrowed, and he tensed. An Angelion? His hands balled instantly into fists. His father's people were at war with the treacherous race.

"Gil, do—" Violette began.

Gil stopped, his wings spreading slightly in shock as he stared at Dev. He held an injector in his hand. It was filled with yellow liquid. This was the man who'd been trying to keep him sedated.

"What did you do?" Gil yelled at Violette. "Quick, get down!"

The injector dropped from Gil's hand as he reached for his waist to grab his gun. Without waiting to assess the full situation, he lifted the weapon and fired. Violette jolted in surprise. Dev didn't hesitate. He grabbed her by the arm and dove out of the way, taking her with him behind a large crate. She struggled against his hold, but he pressed her firmly to the ground to keep her safe.

"Captain?" Gil yelled. Violette moaned an answer.

Dev jumped up to face Gil. He grabbed a high crate and leaped, pulling his weight up to get a better vantage point. As he landed, he saw Gil hovering above the ground. The Angelion swung his arm up. Dev lunged at his target. He slammed into the flying brute, drawing an arm around his neck.

"Stop," Violette yelled below them. Dev wasn't sure which one of them she meant to command.

Gil fired off a shot. It went wild in their struggle, the blast ricocheting off a metal container. Dev swore, thinking of the woman below them. The Angelion was careless. He squeezed the trigger a couple more times. Violette's short cry sounded more annoyed than hurt.

"I said stop! That's an order," she yelled. The men didn't listen. Dev couldn't back down. Gil wouldn't. The war between the Angelion and Bevlon had been raging for a millennium, possibly longer. In truth, neither side could remember how or when it started. Though both races were small in number because of it, none of them stopped the fighting. Dev didn't feel the hatred like his father's people did. The way he saw it, his father's kind didn't care much for him because of his human mother. They used to call him a halfling, a changeling, tainted, half-breed, rotted, spawn... They didn't want to accept him and, well, in return, he wouldn't care about their stupid blood feuds. Evidently Gil didn't get that memo.

"Obey your captain." Dev didn't want to hurt the man, but he would.

Gil's wings flapped, slamming Dev against a wall before lowering him against the sharp edge of a crate. Dev growled as the pain racked over his already sore muscles. Angrily, he reached for the base of a large wing and pulled hard. He heard a loud snap as he broke the appendage. Gil cried out. Dev let go of him as they both plummeted to the hard floor.

He listened for the gun hitting the ground, intent to dive after it. Metal slid against the grated floor. When he landed, he rolled toward the sound. As he came full circle, his forehead pressed into the pointed barrel of a laser.

"That's enough," Violette said, her tone stern. "This is my ship, and I will have order."

"I'll kill you," Gil yelled. "My wing, you demon spawn, you broke my blasted wing!"

"Stow it," Violette ordered. "Or I'll break the other one."

Dev didn't move as he looked up at her. The barrel slid to the bridge of his nose, pressing hard. The captain held a gun on Gil as well. Her hand was steady, lethal. The weapon was an extension of her, and he had no doubt she could use it if called upon.

Violette's eyes turned toward him. "I warned you what would happen if you misbehaved. Give me one reason why I shouldn't eject you from this ship into the black?"

"He attacked me," Dev stated simply. "By the injector he was carrying, I'd say you found your insubordinate."

Violette's hand dropped as she stepped back. He was sure the weapon would rise at a moment's notice. "You have no fear of death, do you? I can see it in your eyes."

"Captain," Gil said. "My wing. He broke my wing."

Violette made her way to the discarded injector on the floor. "You should have considered such outcomes before you brought him on the ship."

"I told you the Bevlon was mine. You didn't protest," Gil held tight to his wing as if he was too frightened to move the appendage.

"And that is why I didn't shoot either one of you just now." Violette eyed the injector. "Is this lethal or sedative?"

"How could you ask that? What fun would it be to kill a Bevlon in a box?" Gil spat, glaring at Dev.

"By the looks of your broken wing, Angelion, it would have been the wisest decision," Dev answered, just as angrily.

"How dare—" Gil began, trying to surge to his feet.

Violette grabbed him roughly by the arm and

plunged the injector into his flesh. He blinked, dazed before passing out onto the floor.

"I could have handled him," Dev protested at her interference.

"This is my ship, and he is my crewman. You'll not be handling anyone." Violette made a move to adjust Gil's wing. She examined the wound. There wasn't a lot of blood, but the support shaft was in two pieces. "This will have to heal naturally. Medical units don't repair broken wings."

"I am aware," Dev answered. He didn't move. His eyes followed the stroking of her hand, oddly aroused by the delicate actions of her fingers, yet jealous of the way she touched the other man. He studied her hands, her wrist, the subtle shift of muscles in her forearm, mesmerized by the movement. For a moment, he let his guard down. A rush of sensations overwhelmed him, and he quickly hardened himself.

Violette struggled to lift Gil but didn't ask for his help. She managed well enough under the dead weight of her burden. Dev sighed, leaned forward to edge her out of the way as he pulled the Angelion onto his shoulder. Violette looked surprised, but she didn't speak as she motioned him to follow her from the cargo hold.

CHAPTER 10

VIOLETTE ORDERED Gil sedated for much longer than was medically necessary. Regardless, Isaac followed her command without question. She had a feeling Isaac would enjoy nursing the unconscious man. Nothing inappropriate would happen, but for Isaac, it would be a fantasy come true to have Gil under his care.

With his wing broken and on a very long natural mend, the Angelion would be in a black hole of a mood. But that wasn't why she didn't want Gil awake. The last thing she needed was the age-old battle between Angelion and Bevlon being played out on her watch. She'd seen the look on their faces. Neither would back down from a fight, and she feared they'd take her ship out in the process.

"There is only room for one fight on this ship,

and that is mine," she swore under her breath, thinking of her father and Josselyn. Though she was a woman always up for adventure, this wasn't exactly the kind of experience she felt like dealing with. Lifting her hand to the door scanner, she opened her quarters and stepped in. Dev stood pretty much where she'd left him, in the middle of the room, black eyes stormy and expression stoic. He filled up the space, intimidatingly so. A small thrill worked over her, filled with a very feminine awareness.

That was something she didn't want to deal with either.

"Gil is being managed," she stated, drawing her mind back to the business at hand. "I contacted Quazer ground, but your friends only spent that one night in the Glamour District before they left the next day. A computer error corrupted their registered travel log."

The side of Dev's mouth twitched up a small degree.

"I suspected that wasn't an error," Violette said in response to the look. "Without it, we have no way of tracking your ship. Unless you know where it's going?"

Dev's expression blanked. "It's hard to say."

Violette nodded. "There are a couple of fueling docks in this part of the X quadrant, but not much else. Unless you insist, I wouldn't recommend you staying behind at any of them. Travel options off the docks are limited, and the accommodations are lacking in everything but space pests."

"What are you offering as an alternative?" The deep, rich tone of his voice gave nothing away.

"I didn't order you brought here, but I am responsible for what happens on this vessel. We'll try to find your ship for you and arrange a meeting—"

"So I can lead you to them?" he inserted.

"Or we can leave you on a planet of your choosing as we fly past. I don't need your help tracking Josselyn. I'll find her."

He stayed quiet.

"Our next stop is to meet up with an HIA ship for a liaison with the Federation." Actually, it was only an offer to join some unit heads in a toast to her father. She didn't have to be there.

Dev didn't move.

"HIA. Human Intelligence Agency," Violette explained.

Dev's brow lifted. She couldn't tell if he was insulted or amused.

"Of course, you know what it is," she said under her breath. "I have no intention of turning you over as a space pirate. However, if you feel it is too much of a risk to—"

"Who said I was a pirate?" He took a step

toward her. The small space felt nearly claustrophobic with him so near. It required sheer will to stand her ground against his menacing figure.

"Your docking reports gave it away." She wished her voice sounded stronger.

"Perhaps we just like our privacy. Perhaps we were worried that someone in a yellow ship would come looking for one of our crewmen. Perhaps this is all an elaborate game set up by you and your crew to either lull me or scare me into some kind of confession. I wouldn't tell you how to find my ship if I even knew where it was. I won't help you find your sister. If Josselyn wishes to seek you out that is her business."

Her eyes inadvertently went to his mouth. She liked the way his lips moved. They were firm, the texture of them begging to be touched. "That is not what I was doing."

"Then perhaps your agenda is political, or religious, or mercenary? You seek to gain my compliance by speaking to me in your soft, feminine way, batting your bewitching eyes and smiling your little seductive smiles. You saw what I was when we landed at Rifflen, and you think to sell me to the highest bidder. You would not be the first to try."

"I do not traffic in…" Her words trailed off. Did he call her bewitching and seductive? "You think I look feminine?"

At that, his guard slipped. Black eyes traveled down her body and back up again. The dark gaze lingered on her hips and breasts a little too long. She felt the tingling warmth of desire erupt between her thighs. The sensation curled around her, flooding her body with the kind of desperate hormonal reaction that would be hard to fight.

"You know the effect you have on men," he stated. It wasn't a question.

"Are you saying I have an effect on you?" She swayed toward him. Her legs shook. This wasn't supposed to be happening.

"Are you trying to get me to confess attraction?" he countered.

Was she? Violette didn't know how to answer that. Well, if she were honest with herself, the truth was she didn't want to think about the answer. "Are you confessing attraction?"

"Are you inviting attraction?"

"Perhaps I should…" Violette glanced at the door. She had to get control of her emotions. "This is my room. If you like, you can stay in here—"

A low growl sounded as he shot forward. Before she could even end her sentence, she was pressed back against the hard metal of her wall by a solid block of pure, hot, male muscle. She moaned. She'd been about to offer the room as his temporary quarters while she bunked elsewhere, but Dev took it more as an invitation to her person. How could she blame him? She had been flirting.

Flirting? Space captains didn't flirt. That couldn't have been what she was doing.

Oh, but then why was she kissing him back? Sliding her tongue into his hot, wet mouth, she let him suck it between his teeth. *Sacre*, but it felt nice the way he flicked his tongue against hers. Heat radiated from his body, warmer than other humanoids. His body hovered close to her, not touching save for their lips. His hands pressed against the metal wall, trapping her before him. There seemed a great fire burning beneath his surface.

Her fingers lifted to his forearms. The fine red lines that decorated his flesh appeared to darken as his kiss deepened. She kept her eyes open, even as they wanted to drift closed. He was staring at her, probing her with his piercing gaze.

She'd wanted him since first seeing him standing on the docking plank to his ship. All the emotions she worked so hard to suppress surged forth—grief, anger, passion, need, they all poured over into him. Their touch became a losing battle for control.

The muscles beneath her fingers flexed as he pulled his mouth from hers. She gripped his arms, not wanting him to stop. Violette opened her mouth to speak, but only a loud gasp escaped her as she drew in a long breath. One of his hands lifted to the front of her tight black shirt. With a jerk, he pulled the neckline and tore the material from her breasts. Her breathing became raspy and her head light.

Heat enveloped her. Violette pressed into the wall. Dev's mouth found her neck as his hand found an aching breast. Her nipple practically exploded against this palm when he touched her. How long had it been since she'd felt the intimacy of a man's flesh? At the moment, she couldn't remember.

There was something to his stoic nature that called to her, a sadness buried deep inside of him, but also a repressed passion that smoldered beneath the surface. If his body heat were any indication, it would do more than simmer once unleashed. She wanted to feed into that passion until his blood boiled like hers. None of this made sense, and yet, here she was, kissing Dev and forgetting about everything rational in her life.

Oh, to feel something beyond sadness and duty. To not have to think.

Her hands moved to his clothing, intent on undressing him. She could feel he was shaped like most humanoid males, yet she wanted to explore the look of him. Bevlons were a rare breed, and this was the first one she'd come across in all her travels. She had heard plenty from Gil's incredibly biased accounts, enough so that she'd been curious to read up on her own. She knew his kind kept to themselves, typically residing on some hot frying pan of a planet.

His body seemed cut from a pliable metal. Solid muscles attested to a life spent in exercise. It was evident by the way he fought Gil that he was trained in combat. There had been a fearlessness in him that captivated her and a borderline recklessness that stirred her curiosity.

Material peeled from flesh until nothing separated them. He didn't speak, so neither did she. Violette worried that the spell between them might break should they utter a word. Something inside her shook free, like a laser missile bursting out of its shell toward another starship, making contact, exploding, destroying itself and its target in the same stellar process. It was hot and dangerous and in many ways stupid, but she couldn't keep away from the flame of that gloriously bright moment. She locked her sights on him, fully aware that the decision she was making was a bad one that could destroy them both, if not physically at least metaphorically. Her crew would never forgive her, especially Gil. They would feel betrayed. They might not even respect her. This man was part of the ship that protected her sworn enemy, even if that enemy was her sister. Not to mention, she could dress up the facts all she liked, but he was technically a prisoner of her ship. Captain and prisoner. On opposites sides of her sworn sense of vengeance. Enemies by every logical rationing of the situation.

But Violette couldn't stop kissing him. He was heat and passion and insanity. He tasted like dark liquor, and his touch was just as intoxicating.

Dev's hands massaged her breasts. She moaned weakly at the sensations flooding her. Thumbs tweaked her nipples into tight buds. Tiny shock-waves found their way down to her pussy. He moaned in the back of his throat. Lips slid from hers as he worked his way over her jaw to her earlobe. He nipped at her ear. Her hands ran through his dark hair, pulling him closer. She angled her throat in offering. He took the invitation, sliding his mouth down her neck. Teeth skimmed her flesh. She tensed, thinking he might bite her. Instead, he drew his tongue in a delicately teasing trail to her shoulder.

Dev's fiery skin and fierce demeanor belied his gentle touch. She wouldn't have guessed he'd be such a tender yet forceful lover. His hands seemed to be all over her body, moving and gliding, caressing and touching every inch of her flesh. He brought his kiss lower, along her collarbone to the valley between her breasts.

Violette stroked his arms and shoulders. Her

fingers found hold in his thick hair. Ah, *sacre*, but his kisses felt wonderful.

She rocked her hips toward him as he moved lower. The hard metal at her back gave her leverage as she pushed her hips forward and spread her legs. He licked her navel before dipping his head between her thighs. Violette gasped. His hot tongue probed the softness of her sex, parting the lips to find the sensitive bud of her clit buried between them.

Violette cried out, unable to hold back. His kissed deepened at her response. He tested her reactions, quickly adapting the movements of his mouth to give her ultimate gratification. Her skin was flushed and her breathing became hard. She slammed her fist against the wall as the pleasure built. A loud, satisfying bang resounded over them so she did it again.

Dev jerked his head back, looking up at her. Those dark eyes seemed filled with the promise of sin, though perhaps it was only her imagination, or the look of his red skin, the stark depths of his eyes.

Violette grabbed a fistful of his thick hair and roughly pulled him to standing. His hands hit on either side of her body to trap her. He breathed hard, each harsh sound puncturing the silence. She still held his locks, pulling at the roots. A low growl sounded in the back of his throat. Her lips parted, and he licked between them, flicking his tongue to dance teasingly along the edges. His hand slid into her hair as he used the locks to jerk her away from the wall. She instantly let go of his hair as he walked her backward to her bed.

Her legs hit the low mattress. Thinking he'd let go, she swept her leg into his in a maneuver to get him on his back. He didn't release her hair, and she ended up falling on top of him. The loud smack of their flesh slapping together sent a tingle over her body. She had never felt so alive in her life. His heat, his taste, his smell, all her senses were overwhelmed.

She began to move over him, straddling his waist. The firm press of his cock slid against her ass. She hadn't looked as they stripped from their clothing. The length of it didn't surprise her. He was such a large man. It made sense that all of him would be in proportion to that fact.

Tiny dark red lines ran haphazard patterns over his entire length, like a tattoo inked in blood. The design was natural, beautiful, mesmerizing. She traced her fingers along the lines. Her actions caused him to tense. He looked down at her hands.

Violette could see the threat of the rational dawning in his eyes. She covered his mouth with her hand before he could speak and quickly maneuvered her body over his. The first intimate contact of his shaft probing into her depths caused her to gasp. She trembled as she forced herself lower. He didn't move, didn't stop her. She lifted and then slowly sat back down. It didn't take long before a natural rhythm struck up between them.

Dev began to thrust his hips, pressing up as she came down. Their actions became almost angry, like a fight both of them could win. His hands slid onto her hips, guiding her over him. She loved the mindlessness of the moment. Pleasure didn't have to make sense, it just was. Before long the tremors of climax were washing over her. She dug her fingernails into his chest. Heat exploded inside her as he came. The eruption was everything she expected it might be—mindless bliss with an aftermath of consequences.

As she pulled off of him, she shivered at the sudden rush of cold air that hit her body. He'd been so warm, and the room's temperature seemed to drop without his touch. She backed away from him. Violette was too practical to ponder senseless things like "What have I done?" and "What was I thinking?". She'd known exactly what she was doing. And now, she was going to have to figure out the best way to minimize the ramifications.

"This never happened," she stated in her most imposing tone. It wasn't the most well done statement, but it was the only one she had.

When in doubt, give an order. Always act as if

you know something the others don't. Crewmen won't question the boss.

The advice had come from her father. For a moment, with Dev, she hadn't thought about any of her responsibilities. Now they came rushing back to weigh heavier on her mind than before.

Violette went to the clothing drawer built into the wall and ran her finger over the scanner. It opened, and she quickly dressed in a tight black shirt and even tighter red pants. The waistband had two narrow strips of material that looped around her waist and over her shoulders to create a decorative pattern on her shirt. When she turned, Dev stood, fully clothed. She hadn't even heard him move from the bed. Searching his blank expression, she could detect nothing in him that would hint at the passion erupting within the room moments before.

"This will be your quarters while you are a guest on my ship. I will make alternative arrangements." Violette moved for the door a little too fast. And, as the metal entryway slid shut behind her, she couldn't help but feel a little disappointed that he hadn't tried to stop her. Then again, what did she expect? The man her crew kidnapped to fall suddenly for the revenge-seeking captain? Theirs really wasn't a fairytale romance in the making.

CHAPTER 11

STANDING emotionless should have been second nature to Dev, but as he watched Violette dress and dismiss him like some paid sex droid he couldn't help but struggle to keep his composure. Everything in him wanted to explode in anger, and the anger was only to cover the hurt. He held back, swallowing the emotions until it choked his throat and tightened his stomach.

What did he expect? Cuddling? Soft words? A smile?

He should be grateful she touched a demon like him at all.

Then again, he'd seen her crew. Perhaps she had some kind of strange fetish. Being a novelty was almost worse than being feared.

Frustration could not erase the feel of her delicate hands from his mind. She'd been forceful and fearless in her passion. He wanted to touch her again, to explore the full length of her body. He needed to hold her, to feel a heart beating against him, steady and without trepidation.

Perhaps that was the cruelest of jokes. He had the Bevlon's body with the human need to be loved. The traits did not belong in the same man.

When he was alone, his hands balled into fists. But, instead of striking out, he kept his muscles tight. Captured, pleasured, dismissed. There was only one thing he knew to do about the undercurrent of frustration flowing beneath his surface. Falling forward onto the floor, he caught his weight and began pressing up furiously in exercise. He'd go until he couldn't lift his body. It was no simulated battle in the VR, but it would have to do.

Dev pushed his overtired muscles until they began to shake with fatigue and then kept going. Only when he collapsed on the floor, breathing hard and completely spent, was he forced to stop. He enjoyed the numbness that came at such a moment, not only in his body but also in his mind. Unfortunately, the feeling didn't last long.

He couldn't help but wonder about his friends. Violette's crew had no reason to hurt a baby so Parker should be safe. Jackson would demand they implement a rescue plan. Jarek would ensure they were smart about it. Rick would make a crude joke to show he cared.

Dev didn't want his friends flying into harm to save him. He didn't wish to risk them to save himself. He would find his own escape before that happened. In a way, the quiet tin can of a room was comforting and familiar. The isolation reminded him to be self-reliant.

He lay on the metal floor, limbs stretched out, cheek pressed to the ridged surface. It was uncomfortable and chilled, and he refused to find anything better. At least now he was no longer squished into a crate. He closed his eyes and evened his breathing. Vibrations along the floor would wake him up if anyone came close to the door.

When he opened his eyes, it was to see legs in tight red pants. Well, more correctly, it was to see in-between legs in tight red pants. He started to smile before he caught himself. Not such a bad view.

Violette sat on the floor. Her back pressed against the door, and her hands draped over her knees as she watched him. Was this an invitation?

"What have you decided?" she asked.

Dev pushed up from the floor. Blast it. Not an invitation. "What makes you think I've decided anything?"

"You're sleeping. You don't strike me as the type to sleep if there is work to be done."

Whatever drugs Gil had managed to get into his system while he was trapped like cargo must have dulled his senses. "And you don't strike me as the type to watch a man sleep. Or are you that starved for entertainment?" He pretended to be unconcerned as he stretched his arms. His muscles were tight and achy.

She motioned to her cheek and then pointed at his face. "You have floor marks on your cheek."

Dev touched his skin, feeling the imprinted texture of his hard bed on his flesh. It would go away. "You have green marks around your waist."

She laughed at the observation. "A teenage indiscretion, an old style tattoo artist, and a stolen bottle of whiskey."

Dev gestured at the darker line on his arm. "Born that way."

She nodded behind him. "You can use the bed."

He glanced over his shoulder. "So can you."

"Quick escape." She pointed her thumb behind her to the door. Though, she hardly looked concerned and there was nothing quick about her position. She'd have to stand to reach the door scanner, and the room was small. He could snap her neck before she even thought of leaving. Of course, he wouldn't.

"This is not who we are." She slowly stood,

keeping an eye on him as she tried to act unconcerned.

Dev arched a brow. He mimicked her previous position, resting his arms on his knees as he sat on the floor and leaned against the frame of the bed. "You're not trying to convert me to some strange calling, are you? Which one is it? We're all pawns to the gods? Do we belong to the space overlords?"

"You're surly when you wake up."

He tried smiling at her. It was a weak effort, but it did cause her to relax her posture. Damn the woman was stunning. He wished she'd smile. Hell, as long as he was wishing for stuff, he wished she'd take off her clothes and let him do naughty things to her again.

"Besides, Salebinaben Johobik en Dehauberkel-sain en Thoraxian en Yyrtolzx Devekin, everyone knows the space overlords are in a battle with the almighty whiteholes. It is our duty to join the fight." Her tone was wry, and it took a moment for him to realize she was teasing him.

"You remembered my full name," he said in surprise.

"What can I say? I'm impressive."

"Your pronunciation could use a little work." He chuckled to lighten the insult. "So, who are we then?"

"We, as in my crew. We are not kidnappers. We

don't ransom or traffic in life. I have no quarrel with you or the other members of your crew. My dispute is with Josselyn."

"Josselyn is a member of my crew." Dev had expected they would eventually have this conversation. He'd much rather be warring with her in bed, but he saw the pain in her eyes. She had to try, and he had to protect his family. Josselyn was now his family. She was with Evan. That is all he needed to know.

"Then she's a new member. I can't imagine she has proven herself very valuable." Violette began to pace.

"Depends on how you define value." Dev stayed on the floor, observing her. He enjoyed watching her move, like a wild animal endlessly looking for a way out of her cage, mind working, seeming to have forgotten she held the key to her own locked door.

"My father. That's how I define value. He was a good man. He fought for alien rights. He was a well-respected general and a humanitarian and an alienitarian and..." She paused, studying him. "Well? Don't you have anything to say to defend her?"

"I know you're grieving, and while I cannot understand, as my father was no one to grieve over, I am sorry you are feeling pain." Dev sighed, hoping she would let the conversation end there. She wouldn't like his true opinion.

"So you admit my father was a good man," Violette insisted.

"No, only that I do not wish to argue that point with you. A good man is who your father was to you."

"Are you saying he wasn't that to everyone else? Because I know hundreds, thousands who would agree with me."

Dev finally stood. Honesty might get him killed, but it looked as if Captain Violette needed a strong dose of it. "And I saw what remains of the settlement on Florencia's Fifth Moon. I saw what was done there, what Jack Stephans had ordered done there. I saw the bodies of the dead shoved into a hole in the floor of a castle and left in a pile to rot. I saw the imprisoned innocent in statue form, blasted apart by lasers in their help-less state, turned to so much dust it coated the room, and at first we couldn't tell what we were stepping on—children, women, men, it didn't matter. They were imprisoned and then killed while helplessly locked in stone. I saw a settlement whose people were turned to stone and their lives coated with ice because the weather regulating satellite was destroyed by Federation blasts. Josselyn was one of those imprisoned. The entire Florencia Moon settlements were wiped out. That is who the general is to those people but I can't bring forward hundreds of witnesses because they're all dead."

"My father would never." Violette shook her head. Her voice rose as she charged toward him. She pointed her finger up into his face. "I won't believe some woman pretending to be my sister. I don't care if we have the same mother genetically. She is not my sister. And your repeating of her lies about the general will not help you gain your freedom."

"I thought I wasn't a prisoner." Dev wasn't sure why he had presented her with the full truth as bluntly as he had. Maybe if she understood, she would give up her revenge. The heat of her expression was centered in her eyes. For a moment, he didn't know if she'd kiss him or hit him. He leaned closer, knowing which one he'd like best. She did neither.

"You're not, but…" She took a deep breath and stepped back. "I want you off my ship."

"I didn't ask to be on your ship."

"That point has been established." Violette regained her composure and eyed him with perfect calm. "Let's not belabor it again."

Her mask didn't fool Dev. He knew well how people hid emotions. By Bravon's fire, he was an expert at it. If she continued to swallow down her grief she'd become a bitter, hollow shell. What she needed was an explosion, a way to release her pain, and Dev needed a fight to bury his. If she yelled at him, struck at him, then maybe he wouldn't feel the desire simmering in his blood.

"You brought it up." Dev crossed his arms over his chest.

Now she looked as if she wanted to throw him off the ship into the black. "You're wrong about the general. He was a good man."

"Good men are sometimes born from bad deeds. Everyone has secrets."

Violette strode to the door. The pain and grief building inside her was too much. On her way out, she stated, "You're wrong. You don't know anything."

CHAPTER 12

Violette stared at Jo in irritation. "I'll pay for the extra fuel burn. I said fly us to the nearest port as fast as we can get there. I want the unauthorized cargo off my ship."

Why were her orders being questioned? It was Gil's fault she had an infuriating Bevlon captive to deal with. Jo was being overprotective of the ship as if putting it at full speed was going to damage the engines. Isaac insisted they let their prisoner starve so that he'd be weakened and more vulnerable and refused to bring Dev food. Ghost…well he just didn't bother to show up when she called to him.

"Your ship," Jo said, stroking his hand along the metal control panel. "But she's my lady."

"I don't even have words," Violette muttered, leaving the cockpit.

"She never lets me down," Jo called after her.

"Just get us to the port!" Violette marched down the passageway to the small dining area. Without much thought, she grabbed a couple of food packs from a crate before turning around to make her way toward her quarters. No one was starving on her watch.

Violette stopped walking and stared down the corridor. She didn't want to face Dev. If she looked at him, she'd want to hit him, then kiss him, then hit him, then kiss him, then yell at him, and then kiss him to keep him from yelling back.

He was wrong about her father. The general was a good man. She'd seen it for herself. She knew of the many missions he took part of to help people. She'd seen the orders he'd signed, and the awards and honors he had received. She'd watched the thank you transmissions.

Violette looked down at the food packs in her hand. Regardless of the fact she wanted to run away and hide, she had a duty to perform. Repeating the words her father said to her on many occasions, she uttered, "Family first. Duty second. Then everything else."

Since her family was dead that left duty. She wasn't a killer or torturer or kidnapper. Dev was in her care and duty demanded that she bring him food and see to his needs. Remembering his heated touch, she shivered and tried to suppress the feeling. "Not those needs, Vi."

She forced her feet to move. The plan was to drop off food and leave.

Drop off. Leave. Drop off. Leave. Drop off…

Violette stopped at the door to her quarters and ran her hand over the scanner. Dev sat on the floor like he merely waited for her to return. His blank expression didn't give any hint as to what he was thinking. The drugs Gil gave him had worked their way out of his system, and there was a new clarity in his gaze when he looked at her. There was no fear in him, which took away any leverage she might have to keep him in line.

"You may sit on the bed." She tossed a food pack at him, and he caught it easily with one hand. "There is no reason for you to be uncomfortable."

Dev studied her for a moment before slowly pushing up from the floor to sit on the edge of the bed. She waited for him to speak and was a little glad when he didn't. There was no reason to continue their previous conversation. She didn't want to fight with him. She just wanted him off her ship and for her life to go back to what it was— seeking revenge.

Violette motioned to the food pack he held, "It's

not fancy, but it's all we have on board." She tore hers open with her teeth and then drank more than ate the thick contents.

Dev followed suit and tilted his head to consume the meal. When he'd finished, he said, "These are like eating fuel sludge runoff. Your father was a general, and you don't have a food simulator on your ship? How do you not have access to that technology?"

"We have a Thinean on board, and he requires a special filtration modification in our life support system. It sends off a frequency that is incompatible with food simulators. The units kept breaking," she explained. "Besides, I was raised on Federation meal packs. One can get used to anything if it's for survival."

"I understand. I was raised with branding sessions to make me tougher."

"You're comparing meal packs to mutilation ceremonies?"

"They both must be suffered through," Dev stated.

She thought he might be making a joke, but he didn't show emotion, so she didn't either.

Her eyes traveled to his skin. There were scars, but most looked like the result of combat, not branding. The red bloodlines moving over his flesh were less noticeable than before. She wanted to ask him to lie down so she could follow them with her finger, tracing them until she could understand the pattern they would form. "You don't look branded."

When she continued to study his arms and neck, searching for the memory he'd mentioned so casually, he stood. Violette took an involuntary step back. Dev dropped the empty pack on the floor next to the bed. He pulled his shirt over his head and tossed it aside. Her breath caught, and she couldn't look away. The desire she had for him bubbled to the surface. His hands reached for his side, and he loosened his waistband.

"What are you doing?" She didn't want him to stop but felt some feeble protest was in order.

Dev did something unexpected. He turned his back to her and lowered his pants so she could see a series of small scars moving down his side and hip. They made a path down to the backs of his thighs. "I'm showing you."

The puckering of strange symbols created a crude pattern in his flesh. Her eyes followed the trail before lifting to his naked ass. Tight muscles flexed. She tossed her empty food pack next to his on the floor and then moved closer. She reached a finger to trace a scar. He stiffened in surprise and glanced back at her.

"How could anyone do this to a child?" Violette glanced at her arm the second the words were out of her mouth. She had her answer. Her father had given her a scar, too.

"Pain conditioning is the Bevlon way." He held still, not bothering to pull up his pants. Her finger traced the pattern across the back of his thigh to his hip. She had not noticed them before in their frenzied lovemaking.

Love? No. What they did was not lovemaking. It was more primal than that. There was no love here. There couldn't be. Violette did not feed into romantic notions. She couldn't afford to. This man was the friend of her enemy. She had to remind herself of that fact. She couldn't forget it. Then why couldn't she force herself to leave?

Nothing in this universe was simple.

Violette felt drawn to him, wanting to be closer, wanting to connect and feel. Flattening her hand more fully against his flesh, she let it slide around to his stomach. She stood next to him and leaned her cheek against his back. Heat radiated off his skin. The intimate contact of flesh made it impossible to pull away. His breathing became hypnotic.

She closed her eyes. "I'm so exhausted."

Why did she admit that? It felt like a weakness.

He turned in her arms. Her head lifted briefly before resting on his chest. Her gaze roamed over his body, traveling over his stomach to the growing arousal between his thighs. He clearly wanted her, but he didn't move to initiate passion.

He rested his hand on her shoulder. "Then you should rest."

Her exhaustion was more than just lack of sleep. It was the weight of everything sitting on her shoulders that she had to face alone. Dev was not part of her life. He was a brief, passing moment. She could never care for him. Life had made sure of that. But for right now, in this instance, she took comfort in the fact that he was warm and breathing, and that she liked the feel of him against her. Before when they came together, it was an explosion. Now, it was...

He ran his hand slowly down her arm, causing her to shiver at the brush of heat.

Now it was something she could not define.

She lifted her head to gaze into his dark eyes. There was a sadness in him, a regret. Did he feel it to—the temporariness of their time together?

Dev kicked off his boots and then stepped out of the pants that were piled around his ankles. He leaned over and lifted her up into his arms. He laid her down on the mattress and then settled next to her, keeping his body on the side closest to the door. The narrow bed would only fit them comfortably if Dev rested on his side. He arranged his arm over her waist and held her against his chest.

"Sleep," he said.

The word sounded like an order, but she didn't protest as she closed her eyes. Yes. Sleep.

CHAPTER 13

EVEN BEFORE DEV lay down beside Violette, he knew he would betray the trust she'd shown him when she'd leaned against his body. The path for a man in his situation was pretty clear. He needed to escape his captors without leading them back to his crew, and before his friends decided to engage in a rescue mission. He didn't want anyone hurt, not over him.

He touched Violette's cheek as she slept. She was still clothed, and he was naked. Her parted lips acted like a lure to his, begging him silently for a kiss. He denied himself. He was good at denying himself. When the urge became almost too much to bear, he made himself picture each member of his crew, even baby Parker, and then he forced himself to imagine their ship exploding in a space battle that did not need to be. He made himself feel it until he experienced the pain fully.

Then he imagined this woman next to him, so stubborn in her cause, so hurt and alone, and he knew what a future of revenge would mean for her. She'd assembled a crew that would most likely give her little by the way of familial affection. There was nothing wrong with that, except humans tended to need some kind of emotional connection or other drives would take over. For Violette, that drive would be vengeance. It would consume her, and she would never stop coming after Josselyn until either or both sisters were dead. And for what? General Jack Stephans? To Josselyn, a century of good deeds would not erase the mass genocide of her people. To Violette, her father was not the man Josselyn had known before going inside her stone prison.

Violette's soft breath tickled is cheek. The lights had dimmed in the room, the timer obviously indicating that it was nighttime on the ship. Still, he waited next to her in the quiet minutes longer than he needed to.

He had one advantage. Josselyn did not want Violette dead or harmed. Whereas Violette would never stop, and the longer she chased her sister, the more ingrained the hatred would become until there was nothing left of her soul.

Revenge would not bring Violette happiness.

Maybe he could change her course. She'd hate him, but he'd give her a chance at a different life. He would save his crew, and hers. Dev would like knowing that she was there, out in the universe, a woman who had once touched him without fear or hesitance. She had done more for him than he could ever explain. With one gentle finger tracing his scars she'd made him feel as if he wasn't a demon. She'd seen him as a man.

In a perfect universe, he'd kiss her now, those parted lips. He'd let her ease the ache in his body. Already his cock was tight with need. But to kiss her now would be a betrayal. She'd given him a single moment that he could hold on to for the rest of his days. And, hate it as she would, he was going to give her the same gift. He would save her from herself before she was too far down the path she was on.

Dev slowly slipped away from her. He dressed as quietly as he could manage. She made a small noise but did not wake. When he was ready, he turned toward the bed. There was no medical unit in the room to help sedate her. He was going to have to use force.

"I know you won't forgive this, but hopefully, you will understand I must do my duty," he whispered, so softly the words weren't really audible. "This is for the best. I'm going to help you change your destiny."

He watched his hand move toward her like it was someone else's. The motion to subdue her was easy, however, forcing himself to perform the task was not. His arm slid under her head and his hand clamped her mouth before her eyelids even fluttered. She struggled in confusion as he lifted her from the bed. Her feet pushed off the mattress in an effort to dislodge his hold. Her fight wouldn't work. She was small and fragile compared to him. All he could do is make adjustments so as not to injure her. One arm secured her waist as he continued to hold his hand over her mouth to muffle the protests.

Violette clawed at his arm and then suddenly stopped. Her head tilted a few times as if becoming aware. She elbowed him hard in the stomach. He grunted in surprise as she struck a rib.

"I don't want to hurt you," he stated.

"*Men mef me mo,*" came her stifled response.

"I can't let you go." He lifted her feet off the ground. "But we have two options. Either we can use the escape pod, or I can take over this vessel. I assure you both tasks are within my skill set. When you started your foolish errand to come after us, I learned everything I could about the model of your ship."

Dev couldn't understand her muffled response, but didn't dare take his hand away. From the tone, he could well guess she was cursing him. Her feet dangled above the ground as he brushed his arm against the scanner to open the door. It took a few times before the device registered what he was doing.

Since he had no desire to steal her ship and subdue her crew, he decided the escape pod was their best bet. "Don't do anything stupid. I don't want to hurt anyone."

He carried her pressed against his front side as he made his way down the long corridor. The ship was laid out to factory standard, and the halls were easy to navigate after his hours exploring the design in the VR room.

Violette wiggled as she tried to loosen his hold on her. He walked faster. Finding the access hatch to the pod, he lowered her to the floor. It was a mistake. She pushed back with her feet, slamming him into the metal wall. Her teeth bit into his hand, and he jerked it away from her mouth.

"I'm trying to help you." He managed to spin the handle on the hatch and pull it open.

"Take the pod and go before the others hear what you're up to. They'll kill you, and I won't be able to stop them." She didn't scream for help but kept her voice quiet. His hold on her waist tightened. "I want you off my ship."

Dev reached his hand into the open hatch and felt around for the hand-held medic unit that should have been anchored to the wall. "I'm working on it."

Finding the unit, he glanced at it to see which model it was before pushing the buttons in a memorized sequence. He pulled it from the wall.

"I'm not after you, Dev. You can let me go. I won't stop you from leaving. All I want is Jossel—"

Dev pushed the medic unit against her arm, and she instantly stopped talking. He caught her and held her to his chest. "I'm sorry it has to be like this, but I can't let you hurt my family."

She didn't hear him. The sedative would make her sleep. Dev leaned over and carried her through the hatch. He placed her hand on the security scanner before programming the pod for a silent escape. The crew wouldn't know they'd left until they were well away from scannable airspace.

He set her gently in the co-pilot chair and strapped her in. The pod was small, almost too small for the both of them. The pilot's seat was a tight fit, but he figured comfort wasn't the designer's primary concern when creating safety features. He began launch sequences and disengaged the pod from the main ship. Then, he programmed the autopilot to head toward the nearest sustainable planet. As far as where they would land it was pretty much luck of the draw. But since pods weren't meant to sustain two people over long distances, it was a chance he needed to take.

"Sit back, relax, and enjoy the jettison through space," he said though Violette wasn't in a condition to answer him.

CHAPTER 14

Erris Settlement, Planet of Murkernal

"You senseless rocketboy," Violette swore in what sounded like drunken garble. She automatically lunged up from her chair to smack Dev across the face. He leaned back, dodging the blow. Swaying on unsteady feet with the lingering effects of the sedative he'd given her, she stumbled against the door of the pod. When he reached to help her, she slapped at his hand. "What did you do?"

"What I had to." The height wasn't designed for a man of his size, and he had to hunch over in the pod. "Don't worry. I'll keep you safe."

She lifted her chin into the air and smashed her hand against her mouth. Drool had slid from her lips. "Ugh, how much did you give me? For the record, I'm not a mammoth."

"Auto inject," he answered. "So whatever dosage was safe."

"You didn't have to do that."

"You would have come with me willingly?" Dev chuckled.

"Fine. You had to do that." Her head cleared by small degrees. "Did you say you'd keep me safe? I don't need you to protect me."

"As you wish, my lady." He gave her a half-smile. Why did he have to be sexy at this moment? She didn't want him to be agreeable or sexy. She wanted him to argue with her so she could hate him.

"Stow it. Calling me that is just bizarre." She sat back down in the co-pilot chair and took several deep breaths. Her limbs tingled, and her muscles felt weak. "I don't even know what I'm doing here. You could have crept off my ship while I was sleeping. And, for the record, I was going to drop you off. There was no reason for you to make me your prisoner. I would have kept my word."

"Yes, you would have let me go. But then you would have tried to follow me to Josselyn. How long until you attempted to imbed some Federation tracker in me? I couldn't trust you not to attempt something. You've made your intentions clear." Dev again reached for the control panel to continue what he'd been doing before Violette failed to punch him. She leaned over to read the viewing screen.

"Why in all the star blazes did you bring us to Murkernal?" Violette closed her eyes. The ship felt as if it rocked, but she knew they had already landed.

"You know this place?" He glanced back at her.

"You don't know this place?"

"It was the closest planet that sustained humanoid lifeforms, and it was marked as non-hostile. We should be right outside a settlement. We'll be able to find somewhere to stay while we wait for my crew to pick us up. Someone will always barter for what we need."

"In the Erris Settlement?" She gave a small laugh. This was almost too perfect. "This would make you the worst captor in history."

"Location looks tame enough," he stated, making his judgment off the specs he was reading. "We should be able to procure food."

"There was food on my ship," she answered, just to be contrary.

Dev ignored the comment. He reached to open the hatch. "Let's go, not-a-lady."

She grimaced. "Food and then what?"

"We wait for my ship to answer my beacon." Cool air blew into the pod as he pushed open the hatch. He reached his hand toward her. "There is not enough fuel for a takeoff, so you might as well come with me and stop trying to come up with an escape plan. I see your mind working. Try to relax and enjoy this vacation away from being captain."

"Oh, I won't need a plan."

"I borrowed your hand for the bio-scanner while you were sleeping. I changed the ship's frequency, and the homing device has been deactivated." He lifted a small yellow unit with wires hanging from it to show he'd ripped the device from the pod. "Odds are like a billion-to-one that your ship will find our new distress frequency before my crew hears it."

Blast it! All right, so she did need a plan.

She tried not to let her irritation show. "Doesn't matter. I can handle myself."

Violette pushed out of her chair, prompting him to open the hatch all the way. Murkernal's surface hardly inspired fear. Tall, slender trees covered in deep green moss enclosed a lush field. Shards of orange-tinted grass reached their waists as they stepped out into the field. Nearby she detected a void in the orange, a narrow walking path cut from one side of the forest to the other.

"Erris Settlement is this way," Dev motioned. He closed the hatch to secure the pod.

Violette smirked. "Don't worry. I'm sure the locals will find us."

Something in Violette's amused expression worried Dev. She appeared confident, but he doubted she'd share her thoughts with him. He glanced around the waving shards of orange, but the field looked empty. According to the pod's records, this planet was friendly enough. No mention of religious zealots. No mention of valuable Federation trade. No mention of fierce beasts. It was just a small planet in a universe filled with small planets. Nothing special.

Dev took a step toward the path, crushing the grass as he moved. Seeds from the stalks brushed onto his clothing. He listened to make sure Violette followed him while keeping himself in front of her to protect her from anything that might come out of the woods. Strange whistling noises started in low, steady tones originating from multiple sources. He glanced back at Violette. She merely smiled at him. That couldn't be a good sign.

He tensed, as the noise grew louder. The grasses began to sway violently along the path. He tried to see what was coming, but the motion turned and came directly at them. Dev reached to grab Violette by the arm and began retreating toward the pod. She cooperated about as much as he could expect.

Her heels dug as she pulled in the opposite direction.

"Now is not the time to be stubborn. Let me protect you. We're fighting blind," he said, more concerned for her than for himself. It was his duty to safeguard her. "Back to a defensive position."

It was too late. The whistling creatures began to encircle them. The grasses parted enough to give hints of pale colors—pinks, purples, soft blues. Violette jerked her arm free and lifted her hands up into the air. She gave a low series of whistles. The creatures moved around her, causing the grass to spread like current. The stalks became only slightly trampled in their wake.

Since the creatures bypassed Violette, Dev took his cue and lifted his arms like she did. But, instead of running around him like a grassy current, he felt miniature hands grab hold of his pants.

"Ooo," tiny voices said in unison before breaking off into a chorus of, "You brought us a big one," and, "Welcome, strangers."

Round heads emerged from the weeds as the locals climbed his legs, almost fighting each other in their excitement to look at him. Slender arms pulled up narrow bodies. The colors he'd seen were the fuzzy hair on their heads. When they weren't speaking in the Old Star language he could understand, they were making the whistling noises.

"Big."

"Stranger, welcome."

"Big."

Violette's laughter rang out over him. He glanced over to her. "Stellar job protecting me, by the way." She grinned and moved about the grasses, looking down to watch where she stepped. "Told you that you were the worst kidnapper ever."

"Where are you going?" Dev shook his leg, not wanting to hurt the little aliens, but unsure how to get them to stop licking orange grass seeds off his pant legs. The bizarre show of affection was making him uncomfortable. "Don't leave me."

"Aw, look, they like you." Violette continued moving toward the path. "I think you made friends."

"So big." One had crawled to press his face close to Dev's. Large eyes tried to gaze into his. Tiny fingers held his cheeks. "A welcome stranger."

"Violette," Dev said, the word more like an order than a plea. "Help me."

"No," she answered.

"Yes, greetings," Dev muttered, pulling the hands from the sides of his nose, and then from his chin, and this ear, and then fingers from reaching inside his nose. He was too scared to move, afraid he'd accidentally hurt one of them. To Violette, he yelled, "Why aren't they scared of me?" before adding almost desperately, "Tell them I'm a demon. Tell them I eat souls. Violette, please!"

Being feared would be easier than this.

"I don't think they care." Violette made it to the path. "I'd like to point out that I could escape right now."

Dev tried prying a pair of hands off his chest. Once he released them, another set landed in their place.

"Do you really want my help?" she asked.

"Yes," he stated without hesitation.

"Then say that I'm the superior adversary."

"What?" The stimulus of many hands on his body wasn't something he was used to. They were petting him, caressing him, licking seeds off him and off each other.

"Tell me I'm superior," she stated again.

"Fine. You're superior. You bested me. You could escape right now." Dev was about two seconds away from shaking the creatures off his body by force. "You're attractive and smart and superior and—"

"Now apologize for drugging me."

"I apologize," he answered. "I should have found a better way."

Violette gave a whistle. The locals stopped pawing at him and turned their attention toward her. "We're here to help."

Violette continued to whistle a song as she strode down the path. The little creatures smiled as they climbed off Dev and then ran through the field to follow her. They disappeared beneath the taller stalks only to emerge on the pathway emitting their low whistles. Dev followed slowly, pushing blades of grass so that he didn't accidentally step on a straggler.

He rubbed his arms, trying to erase the feeling of being pawed. The pastel-headed creatures followed Violette, skipping on narrow legs and swinging slender arms. The strange musical noise they made appeared to squeeze from their lungs with each step, whistling out of the bumps of their noses. They emanated a kind of pure joy he'd never seen.

"Violette," Dev called after her, wanting to catch up.

"Worst kidnapper ever!" she yelled back, not breaking stride.

CHAPTER 15

Before today, Violette had only seen pictures of the Murkernal natives in her father's archives. Part of her lessons had included alien cultures. She always had the impression he wanted her to be a Federation diplomat. Instead, she captained a crew and made space runs as an independent contractor. When the general had been in charge of Rifflen, she was also allowed certain privileges on the base that most civilians wouldn't have access to. It was how Dev was able to obtain Federation records inside her pod about the planet that he might not otherwise have been able to see.

When they held still, the Murkernals looked like sticks in woven jumpsuits with a round ball for a head on top. They were a harmless, playful race on a planet that had no real value to anyone but them.

They also had a fondness for any traveler bigger than they were. Dev, being of considerable size, naturally caught their eager attention. For a moment, she'd considered running off while he was swarmed. She suspected he wouldn't hurt the locals. Despite his gruff manners, he was very gentle with them. It was his pleading, helpless eyes, in the midst of all their friendliness that had made her stay.

Earlier, she hadn't stopped to wonder about how he stiffened for a fleeting second each time she touched him. Seeing his expression in light of the Murkernals playfulness, she felt sorry for him. He wasn't used to receiving affection.

Even now, the natives followed him around their small village, gazing up at him, trying to hold onto his pant legs. They made it difficult for the big demon man to walk. Violette found it adorable.

Evening skies cast the planet in a red and orange light. Streaks of purple outlined the horizon. There were no homes, no buildings, no communication towers, only low-hung canopies that stretched over a clearing and inadequately hid a wooden door on the ground. Dev couldn't have picked a more out of the way location to elude her crew. Who would think to look for them here?

"How exactly are we here to help?" Dev asked. Before she could answer, the natives ran to a large tree and lifted their arms, jumping excitedly. They were too short to reach the branches, and when they tried to climb the slick trunk, they slid down.

Violette exchanged a look with Dev before nodding toward the tree. He slowly approached, hesitated, and then gently grabbed a local with blue hair and lifted him up. The whistling became more pronounced as the Murkernal kicked his feet in excitement.

Violette stepped back from the gathering crowd, not taking her eyes off Dev. The local reached into the tree limbs to retrieve a large berry. He jerked impatiently as Dev lowered him back to the ground. Instead of lifting another one, Dev reached into the tree and began picking fruit. He handed the food down to his enthusiastic followers, who then ran away to eat. When everyone had been fed, she approached Dev.

"You've made the settlement very happy." She reached into the tree and took a piece of fruit. She sniffed it but didn't eat.

"This planet is…" Dev glanced to where the Murkernals scrambled under the canopy. They beat their feet against the ground, digging a hole straight down to bury their bodies until only their heads were above the earth. Cheeks moved as they sucked the fruit. Dev tilted his head to better see them. "I have seen many races, but these—"

"Murkernals," Violette supplied.

"—Murkernals are very strange beings."

"I think they're cute." Violette tossed the fruit into the air in front of him. Dev automatically caught it. "I'm not sure we should find food here. I'll stick with the foil packs."

"Scared?" He arched a brow and made a move to bring it to his mouth.

"Smart," she corrected. "I've seen what the Da'Na virus in non-regulated food can do to a person. You might like liquefied insides, but this," she gestured impishly to her face, "is too pretty for stink pustules."

Dev grinned and placed the piece of fruit on the ground, leaving it uneaten.

"I'm going to the pod," she said. "I'll be back."

"How about I go with you?"

It wasn't a request. She chuckled. "Worried I'll reset your communication signal?"

Violette had thought about trying. She might even succeed in doing so. However, she had an excellent reason not to. This adventure gave her the chance to find Josselyn when his crew came to retrieve him.

"No." He nodded that she should walk.

"If I were going to try to fly the pod, I would have left earlier." She leaned over to look under the canopy to the contented heads poking out of the ground. Violette took a deep breath. She envied the odd simplicity of the Murkernals. One visiting giant handed them pieces of fruit and they were ecstatic. She couldn't imagine anything that would make her that happy. She looked up at Dev. Maybe he'd give her a slice of happy-fruit. "Would it be so bad if I stranded you here? You could live like a god."

He again gestured that she walk with him. "I already have a job."

For a moment, she had forgotten who they were. Her smile fell some, and they walked in silence over the path to the field of orange grasses. The pod was just as they'd left it. Violette grabbed foil packs out of a side compartment. Dev took the emergency kit.

"There has to be something we can eat besides sludge," Dev muttered, eyeing the packs. "I never thought I'd say I miss a food simulator."

"At least, these have nutrients. Simulated food. The name says it all." Violette wasn't sure why she was defending the foil pack of all things.

"Forgive me. I did not mean to insult your childhood traditions." Dev swept his feet as he walked, looking through the grass as they made their way back to the darkening path.

"That's very kind of you." The words sounded sarcastic, even though she didn't mean them to. Violette wanted to say more but over-thought every word before it made its way out of her mouth. She was used to conversations where she either gave orders or argued a point. "Back on the ship, you said something about your father not being anyone to grieve over. Why is that? Was he a bad man?"

"He was a full-blooded Bevlon." The statement was simple as if that should fully explain his past.

"And your mother?" He'd called himself humanoid when he was trapped in the crate, but Violette wanted to know more. The man kept his emotions close, but she saw the pain in his eyes.

"Human."

"I guess I don't understand. So, being Bevlon means you don't mourn the dead?" Violette couldn't imagine. She missed her father every day.

He sighed heavily and studied her. "What are you asking?"

"I'm trying to…" Violette gave a helpless gesture. She was about as good at these get-to-know-you conversations as he was. "I don't know. I'm trying to make conversation, trying to understand why you are the way you are. Were you close to your parents? Were you happy as a child? Are they alive?"

"Oh." That seemed to surprise him, as if no one had ever asked him such questions before. She found that sad. "My, ah, mother's people, humans, they tend to think I am too fierce, a spawn of the devil, the reincarnation of Ancient Old Earth's demons, that kind of thing. So they really don't have much to do with me."

"That doesn't make sense to me," she answered. "It isn't as if aliens are a foreign concept in the universe."

"True, but Bevlons just happen to look like the old earthling version of pure evil, and it doesn't help that my paternal race as a whole are self-serving and cruel."

"But surely your mother didn't feel that way. I mean, she had you, so that means she had to accept who your father was."

"I'm unclear how it happened. After my birth, my mother wanted nothing to do with her demon baby. The last I heard she'd wed a human charm-preacher and settled on some remote planet. I have no memory of what my mother looks like, and my father refuses to give me so much as her name. For all I know, she is married to the Data Moon Brimstoneman who tried to have me sacrificed several years back."

She started to laugh at the obvious exaggeration, but then stopped. "You're not kidding, are you?"

He shook his head. "No. It's how I came to be with my current crew. They saved me from the fire."

"Fire? I thought Bevlons liked the fire."

"Fire hurts, but it won't kill me directly. Intense heat will dehydrate me over a period of several agonizingly painful days. Accounting for that fact, the Brimstoneman had me dragged over sharp rocks to tear my flesh. A Bevlon's skin can survive flames, but our insides cannot. If the zealots had any kindness, they would have tried to drop me into freezing temperatures so that death would come swiftly."

"So then you were raised by your father, like me," she said.

"Yes, I was, but not like you. Because of my mixed heritage and lack of hooves and horns, the Bevlons thought I wasn't demonic enough. They accused me of being too tame and put me through trials to toughen me. When I was of age to do so, I left."

Violette wanted to reach out to him, to pull him into her arms, but refrained. Dev clearly had no place in either culture. She couldn't imagine such a life. No wonder he was so close to his crew.

The sun had almost set behind the horizon. Bright stars gave light to see by. Once at the settlement, Dev put the kit on the ground and pulled out a collapsible emergency ladder. She watched as he secured it to a fruit tree branch.

Soft, steady whistles came from under the canopy as if the creatures slept. "Do you think they wait around for tall visitors to feed them?"

He picked an orange seed off his pant leg. "I think they eat grass and probably wait for food to fall on the ground. If they were gluttonous, the one I put into the tree would have taken more than his fill, so I think there is no harm in giving them better access to—"

Her lips cut off his words. Violette wasn't sure what prompted her to act, but she kissed him.

Dev pulled back in question.

"Come closer," she whispered.

"There are rules about prisoners." He glanced to the sleeping aliens.

"Just a little bit closer," she insisted. "The night is cool, and you are warm."

"I am trying very hard to resist you." He swayed in her direction.

"I wish you wouldn't." She licked her lips, noticing how his eyes kept dipping down to look at them. "You're a very rules kind of man, aren't you, Dev?"

He nodded. "I have certain codes I live by."

"Closer." She kept her voice soft as she leaned into him. "We all have codes, rules, duties."

"We are on opposite sides of—"

"Of?" She touched his chest, sliding her fingers over the hard ridges of his muscles.

"Of..." He glanced down, and she drew her hands up to cup his face and turn his gaze back to hers.

"Come closer." The more he tried to resist, the

more she wanted him. She saw the struggling in his expression, knew that he wanted to deny himself the pleasure they shared.

Violette gripped his face tighter. The heat of him drew her to lean fully against his body. This made more sense to her than conversation. What could she say that wasn't already said? He wanted to protect Josselyn. She needed to honor her father with revenge. This was not a point on which they would meet. Even so, take away that fact, and she was left with wanting to kiss him.

Rigid control over her emotions only kept her desire for him at bay for so long. In that they were the same. But, there were no eyes on them here, not that she cared if people found out she'd had sex with a Bevlon. She did care about her crew thinking she was going soft.

"Closer," she demanded in a part growl.

Dev finally returned her kiss. He cupped her ass and lifted her off the ground in one swift movement. Her nerves tingled where they touched and ached where they didn't. She wrapped her legs around his hips. He walked her away from the canopy, only to go to his knees when they were hidden from view behind the fruit tree.

Firm ground pressed against her back, and she unwrapped her legs. The hunger grew. With every brush of his clothing, the frenzy inside her built.

When she touched him, she felt alive. Her breath quickened. She clawed at his pants to strip the material off him before moving to wiggle out of her own. No man had ever driven her to such a chaotic need. This was a primal dance they both understood.

He pushed the back of her leg, lifting her thigh to kiss the sensitive flesh leading from her knee to her sex. She ran her fingers through his dark hair. The natural heat made the trail of his mouth unmistakable, and with each kiss, she tensed with growing need. Moisture gathered in her pussy. Her toes curled in anticipation. She tried to force his head to her sex, but she could no more move him than she could change the rotation of a planet.

Violette bit her lip to keep quiet. She doubted the natives would be moving around anytime soon, but this is not how she wanted to be caught. Her hips lifted and gyrated as if with a mind of their own. Her legs worked against his shoulders, hooking him the best she could manage to urge him closer.

Lips finally met the sensitive flesh of her sex, and she inhaled a sharp breath. Intense heat added to the pleasure of his wet kisses. Her heels dug into the ground. Hands roamed her thighs and stomach. She was aware of him and only him. An ache built inside her, centering on his mouth.

Violette pulled his hair. Dev obeyed her plea and crawled over her body. His handsome face hovered over hers. She ran her hand under his shirt to his back. His muscles shifted. The pant of his breath tickled her cheek. The depths of his dark eyes bore into hers. Deep emotions were buried there.

Slowly he entered her, each second filled with the promise of completion. She lifted to kiss him, but he drew his lips beyond her reach and continued to stare into her eyes. In that moment, she understood what he sought. He wanted her to know who she was with, who was giving her pleasure. It was a desperate need that she should see him for what he was—a self-proclaimed demon.

But Violette did not see a demon when she looked at Dev. She wasn't frightened by him, or repulsed. In fact, it was quite the opposite. She was attracted to him on a primordial level. He was gravity, and she was a helpless meteor being drawn into his orbit. They crashed together as he slid fully into her depths. She gasped as he rocked his hips into her. The stars danced behind his head, framing his dark hair with their bright light. Rarely had she seen stars so big from the surface of a planet.

"I wish we could stay," she whispered. "Never leave."

Dev's head tilted back as he quickened his pace. Climax hit them in unison. She tensed, trembling as pleasure washed over her. He stiffened above her, a beautiful statue of masculine perfection. After a long moment, he drew his head down to look again into her eyes.

"The rest of the universe doesn't matter here," she said, not really thinking of how much she revealed to him. They were joined in ways beyond that of their physical bodies. "Reality doesn't matter here."

"Ugh, fellas, I'm not sure Dev wants to be rescued."

Violette blinked in confusion at the loud male voice. It took her a moment to realize that three of Dev's crewmen stood nearby. They averted their gazes as if to give them a moderate amount of privacy. None of them were Josselyn's husband.

"Maybe we should come back later," the intruder continued. "Let a guy finish up."

Violette was wrong. Reality did matter here. It had come to find them, just as it always would.

CHAPTER 16

DEV QUICKLY ROLLED off of Violette and adjusted his pants while attempting to shade her with his body from Rick, Jackson, and Lochlann's view. Under normal circumstances, he'd have been pleased to see his friends. Considering the compromising position he had Violette in, their timing could have been much better.

"So, are we saving him or…?" Rick covered his eyes but peeked through his fingers.

"Rick," Dev warned.

"Dev?" Jackson arched a brow to reveal his concerns.

"There are only the two of us," Dev answered. Then, gesturing in the direction of the canopy, he added, "Well, us, and the native whistlers."

"Wait, I know her," Rick exclaimed. "Dev, that's

Violent Violette. She's the one who wants to kill all of us. Dev, you're doing Josselyn's sister?"

Dev glared at the man and opened his mouth. Before he could answer, Lochlann ordered, "Stop talking, Rick, if you know what is good for you."

"All I'm saying is that Dev is the man," Rick muttered. "It was a compliment."

"I am *Captain* Violette," Violette answered. All gentleness left her tone. Dev resisted the urge to look at her. "I do not want to kill everyone. I am not Josselyn's sister. And I am not violent."

"Dev, what does this mean?" Lochlann asked, glancing at Violette.

"I escaped." Dev wondered how to describe what he had with her. What he wanted to say, and what her take was on their relationship, were probably two very different ideas. "I took her with me."

"Her crew?" Jackson queried.

"We used the escape pod. They didn't follow us," Dev answered.

"Good," Jackson stated. "Now perhaps we can end this."

"What?" Violette gasped. She stepped quickly to where the emergency kit was on the ground and searched inside it while keeping her eyes on the men. She withdrew a hand-held medic and arched her hand back as if she would throw it at them.

"Dev gave me his word that I would be protected. No one is going to end me."

Jackson arched a brow and drawled, "I meant end the fight between you and your sister, not end your life. If I were going to kill you, I'd have done it already. Josselyn asked us not to."

"And where exactly is this sister of mine? I'd like to thank her personally for that consideration." Violette smiled, but it didn't reach her eyes. The men didn't answer. She shrugged and let the smile fall. "Worth a try."

Violette lowered her arm. Her expression hardened. He wished he could pull her aside for a moment of privacy, or rewind and freeze time to the minutes before Rick interrupted them. There was much he wanted to say to answer her words, *"I wish we could stay. Never leave. The rest of the universe doesn't matter here. Reality doesn't matter here."*

Dev wanted to erase the hardness from her eyes, but now was not the time and he wasn't equipped to talk about emotions. All he could do for her was try to change her life's course. That was his plan in taking her. That is what he'd continue to do. "Is the ship nearby?"

"I parked it in—giant spaceholes what in the bloody nova is that thing?" Rick pointed behind Dev.

Dev turned to find one of his Murkernal friends

hopping toward him carrying a baby Murkernal in his arms. Soon, the others emerged from beneath the canopy, all holding infants and whistling happily. Dev glanced up to the fruit, and then to Violette, before looking once more at the natives. Apparently, the food he'd given them had extra special side effects.

"No, seriously, what are those things?" Rick demanded.

"Murkernals," Dev said.

"Dev's been planting seeds," Violette supplied. "Ah, congratulations, Devekin, I think you're a daddy."

"Exactly how long were you on this planet?" Rick asked, snickering.

"The ship," Dev demanded. He lifted his hand to gesture politely at the locals even as he stepped away from them. He didn't want them to get excited and try to climb him again. To Violette, he muttered, "I'm really glad we didn't eat the fruit."

"How about we find that ship of yours? I don't want to catch what they have," Violette answered. Her eyes turned to where they'd had sex moments before.

Dev nodded. Even though her comment made a small twinge in his gut, he knew she was right. Of course, he didn't want to get her pregnant. That would be impractical given their circumstance, and he knew how hard it was to raise a baby on a space-ship. Then why was he feeling so…

"Thank you, stranger, thank you," one of the cheery, little, bouncing beings said.

Dev frowned. "Time to go."

CHAPTER 17

WELL, Violette got what she wanted. She'd wanted to remain kidnapped so she would be brought onto Dev's ship, and that's exactly what happened. Unfortunately, her "sister" wasn't on board. The murderer couldn't hide forever. She'd find Josselyn and the next time she wouldn't hesitate to do what needed to be done. The weakness she'd felt on Quazer could not happen again. She shouldn't have let Josselyn walk away.

Apparently, fearing what might await them on the rescue mission to get Dev, the crew dropped off the captain, his wife, and their son, as well as Evan and Josselyn. Violette couldn't imagine trying to raise a baby with her lifestyle. Maybe someday having children would be a possibility. She glanced at Dev. Would they even make good parents?

They? Violette turned her eyes away. She couldn't think like that. They were not a "they". The ache inside her grew stronger.

Violette desperately wished she could pick up a communicator and call her father. She wouldn't tell him she was having relationship issues, but it would be great just to hear his voice. Now she was alone with no one to call when she was having a bad day. It's not like Isaac would want to chat about her feelings.

"Are you hearing me?" Dev asked, studying her from across the small table in the common area. He'd been trying to justify what Josselyn had done. Violette was sure the woman had her reasons, but those reasons didn't change the fact that a good man was dead. Sighing, he continued, "Do you not trust my word? If so, I will stop speaking."

"I believe you believe her lies," Violette stated.

"I do not."

He crossed his arms over his chest and leaned back in his chair. She felt the divide between them but didn't know how to conquer it. When they were together, alone, kissing and touching, she experienced their deep connection. In those moments, there was clarity. In the seconds after that clarity left her, and she felt emptier than before.

Duty. That is what she needed to remember.

Dev did not love her. They were on opposite

sides of the blood oath she'd sworn to her dead father. Wishing to change that fact would do no good and only made the ache inside her chest worse. He was close, right there within touching distance, and yet she could not have him, not all of him as she wanted. The sorrow that filled her made her want to cry out, but she held the emotion in.

Family first. Duty second. Then everything else.

She glanced around the metal common area. The ship was larger and much nicer than hers. It looked like an older model decommissioned by the Federation.

"Got it," Rick stated, strolling into the room with an old holo-box. She wasn't sure what to make of the pilot. He seemed careless and light, but she had a feeling his jokes were a mask hiding something much deeper. There were fleeting moments as they walked back to the ship that his guard had fell when he thought no one watched to reveal sadness in his eyes. Seeing her looking at him now, he questioned, "How's it going…Velvet Violette?"

"No," Violette stated in response to the new name.

"Vengeful Violette?"

"No," she repeated.

"Ah, no worries." Rick winked. "I'll keep working on your pirate name, starbeam."

Dev stiffened and grabbed the holo-box from Rick. "I will launch you into deep space."

"Message received, mission command." Rick loosely saluted Dev and then plopped down on a chair several feet away.

"The captain's wife found this hidden in the ducts of the ship." Dev set the box down. "I thought you might like to see it."

Violette had a feeling she already knew who was on the holo-box. She reached forward and activated it. The miniature image of her father appeared in his shiny white uniform. He looked younger than when he'd recorded the first holo-box she'd found of him. The holograph caused an unexpected flood of emotion. Tears burned her nose and threatened her eyes. She held them back.

"Top secret. Prisoner two, two, five release order number six, nine, twelve. This is General Stephans of the New Earth Settlement on Florencia's Fifth Moon." The holographic image paused before stating, "This is General Stephans of what was *formerly* the Earth Settlement on Florencia's Fifth Moon and this is an official order of release authorized by my superiors and hereby given to the commanding warden in Ice Complex Five, Authorization code H forty-seven, fifty-one. When the ice storms came nearly forty years ago, many of my men were killed. It was too cold to stay and finish our work releasing certain political prisoners and we abandoned post on supreme orders. However, there are a few who remain that should not, as they have been pardoned for their crimes. Attached is a list of prisoners set for immediate release. They will be hostile and should be escorted and left on the Rifflen base in the V Quadrant. No provisions beyond those orders are necessary."

Violette waited as the holographic image faded. She missed that voice. She missed knowing he was out there in the universe.

"The general commanded that Josselyn be freed. She should not have been imprisoned to begin with, but you can, at least, see that she was pardoned." Dev hesitated before reaching across the table to take her hand. "She's not a criminal."

"All this proves is that my father ordered her released." Violette studied the red fingers against hers.

"It proves he had her locked on Ice Complex Five," Rick stated, oddly serious. "Though if you saw the complex, you'd know what that place really is. Just a fancy name for—"

"Florencia's Fifth Moon," Violette supplied, not wanting to hear whatever nickname Rick came up with for the Ice Complex. "I know. My mother was from there. They were part of a human culture preservation project of Old Earth living history—a place for humanoid schoolchildren and bored tourist to go on vacation. Medieval period or something they called the Fifth Moon. The project went defunct. The settlement was abandoned, and the Federation used the location for an ice prison."

"Defunct?" Rick snorted. "That's one way of putting it."

"It stopped earning money, and they abandoned it. I read the historical report on the moons. It's sad, but those things happen. How else would I put it?" Violette glared at the man. She knew she was spoiling for an argument, and he looked as good as a place to start as any.

"Oh, I don't know, maybe that the weather satellites were purposefully destroyed, throwing the moon into an inhabitable state, mainly to hide the crime of a mass genocide from the rest of the universes because—"

"Rick, don't you have a ship to fly?" Dev interrupted the brewing dispute.

"Autopilot," Rick answered.

"Then you're saying we don't need to keep you on board?" Dev arched a brow in warning.

"You're grumpy when you're getting laid," Rick muttered. He stood and moved for the door. "I'm going for food, but don't think I'm bringing you back anything after you threatened to eject me from the ship."

Violette waited until Rick left them alone. "Why show me this recording, Dev?"

"To explain why I'm taking you to Ice Complex Five. Why you need to go there to see it. I want you to consider that revenge may not be the answer you're looking for." He nodded toward the box. "The real answers may lie there, in the past."

"Why did you release Josselyn?" Violette pulled her hand away from his instantly missing the contact of his skin to hers. Even now, with the pain mixing inside her chest, she desired to move closer to him. She wanted to sit on his lap and have him hold her. She longed to kiss him until there was nothing remaining but a rush of pleasure. "It wasn't for your people to do. If you had left her there, we wouldn't be here right now having this conversation."

A different wave of pain washed over her. If they had left Josselyn to rot, then her father would be alive, but then she would have never crossed paths with Dev. That thought stung. Her life had been so empty before Dev came into it. Strange, but very true.

"Because the idea of someone trapped inside stone for a century due to a lost communication was an unbearable option," he said. "We had no choice. I would like to think you would have done the same thing."

The truth was, she probably would have. Or she would have at least told her father about the prisoner and let him deal with it.

Dev stood. "Would you like food? Or would you like me to show you to where you can sleep?"

"Sleep." Violette doubted she could keep any food down. The knot her in stomach and thoughts churning in her head would make it impossible. Her eyes strayed to the holo-box and to the memory of the man it showed. "I'd like to sleep."

CHAPTER 18

Dev escorted Violette to the captain's quarters where she would be staying. Intermediate bands of light shone over her face, brightening and darkening her features with a steady pattern. She held her emotions close, like a trained soldier. Only, she wasn't Federation. He wondered what manner of life she must have had, being raised motherless by a general. That fact explained much about her personality. She had discipline, a strong sense of loyalty, and the kind of single-minded purpose one often found in Federation types. And yet there was a rebellion in her too, a wild need for adventure.

"After Gil kidnapped me, Captain Jarek and his wife decided it would be best if they took their infant son back to his home planet where he would be safe. You may stay in their room, if you like." He regretted not being able to say goodbye to Captain Jarek, Mei, and baby Parker, but he understood why they'd left the ship. None knew how permanent of a move the trip would be. "Lochlann is acting captain, but he already has a room."

The captain's quarters was the largest room on the ship, and much bigger than her quarters on the *Racing Banana*. Mei had decorated the walls with strips of yellow and red silk embroidered with her home planet's flowers. They stirred at the gentlest of air current, like the opening of a door.

"I hope you'll be comfortable here." Dev wished he knew what to say to erase the sadness from her features.

"Don't want me bunking with you?" Violette glanced around and appeared uncomfortable. "Afraid I'll escape and take you as my prisoner? It does seem to be my turn."

This woman had no idea how much he was her prisoner, even now, while on his ship surrounded by his people.

"My quarters will not fit both of us. I thought you might be more relaxed in here." Dev waited for her to invite him to stay, or to yell at him from forcing her to be on the ship, or to say anything at all to reveal how she felt about him. When she didn't, he stepped backward out of the door. "The computer call button will find me if you need assistance. I will be nearby. Don't bother contemplating an escape. Our pod is damaged, and if you don't know Lucien's system, you'll never figure out how he rigged the communications to work."

"Can't promise that I won't try." She stared at the bed, not moving.

"We're not locking you in a cage, so please don't hurt anyone on this ship." Dev lifted his hand to the sensor on the wall.

"I don't want to hurt anyone but the one who deserves to be brought to justice," Violette answered as the door closed her inside.

Dev shut her in the room and pressed his hand lightly to the metal barrier. He wanted her so badly it hurt, and yet he had to suppress his feelings. Turning, he strode until he was at Evan's quarters. He knocked. It only took seconds for the door to slide out of the way.

"Did you show her?" Josselyn eagerly asked as if she'd been waiting by the door.

"Yes. I showed her," Dev answered.

"Then she saw my pardon and the holo-box the general left me on Quazer. That has to sway her some, doesn't it? It's part of the truth from her father's own lips." Josselyn looked past Dev as if she'd find her sister in the hallway. "Will she talk to me? Is she in the commons?"

"Lochlann told her you were not on the ship. I

believe that is best for now." Dev sighed. "I'm sorry, Josselyn. I don't know that she will ever listen to what we have to say, so we must show her. Then, you can try to speak to her."

Josselyn nodded. "I understand. Let her roam the ship. I'll stay hidden. I want her to trust us, not feel like a prisoner. My mother would have wanted us to be sisters. My father would have wanted whatever made my mother happy. I intend to do everything I can to honor what would have been their wishes."

Dev gave a soft smile. "You're more like Violette than you can imagine. It must be a Craven thing. You both are so certain of things, and so stubborn in your views."

Evan tilted his head, edging closer. Dev knew that look. Evan picked up on the emotions Dev tried to hide. Dev attempted to harden himself to his friend's psychic probing.

"Please be careful." Josselyn gave him a smile, but the expression didn't reach her eyes. "When I hired her to give me a ride to Rifflen, before I knew who she was to me, she was very convincing in her part. She knew who I was from the beginning, and I never suspected a thing."

"I will be careful, my lady," Dev said dutifully. His words seemed to ease her worry some, and she nodded.

"Dev?" Evan asked, holding his chest. "Are you well?"

"No," Dev answered. There was no reason to lie. As an empath, Evan knew the truth already. "But I am on the only course I can be on."

"Dev, I have never felt this strong of an emotion in you before. Is this true?" Evan stepped cautiously closer. He reached out his hand as if to touch Dev's chest but stopped short and placed his palm over his own heart. "You have fallen in love with Violette?"

Love? Dev looked at the floor. He would never have named his feelings out loud. He was a beast, a demon, and now a kidnapper. When he forced Violette to see what her father was, she would forever associate him with that truth. He wasn't made to be loved. Violette accepted him as a lover, but as someone she could love? No. His was a one-sided heartache.

"Dev?" Josselyn questioned when he didn't speak.

"Yes," Dev answered simply. "But she doesn't love me back, so there is no reason to discuss it."

Evan nodded. He looked as if he'd say more, but Dev left before he could. Nothing Evan had to say would ease the sorrow he felt.

Yes. He loved Violette, but he had not wanted to give his pain a name. Put fifty yorkins in front of him and he'd slaughter every last one of them. But set a beautiful woman with soft brown hair and a fierce demeanor before him and he would lose to her every time.

Demons didn't get to be loved like that. That was not how the universe worked.

CHAPTER 19

VIOLETTE WASN'T sure how she slept, but she did. For some reason when Dev told her she was safe, she felt safe. She half hoped she'd wake up to find him next to her, or even in the room silently watching over her. He wasn't. She woke up alone.

When she had lay on the bed, the lights had dimmed. The way that the sensors were set made it impossible for her to tell how long she'd dozed. By the growling protests of her stomach, it had been a long time.

As she stretched, she glanced at the call button that would bring Dev to her. She wanted to see him, but purely for selfish reasons that had nothing to do with the practicality of her current situation. Instead, she opened the door and peeked out into the metal corridor. Since this ship model used to be

Federation, she could determine the basic layout fairly easily. She needed to find communications. Even though she was hungry, she could put off eating. Work first, everything else later.

The communications room was easy to find. However, the control panel was far from Federation issue. Determining the frequency controls proved simple, but the rest of the unmarked switches were a challenge. She ran her finger over the scratched surface where the control's labels should have been etched.

"Thing of beauty, isn't it?" A man leaned against the door frame, watching her.

It took Violette a moment to remember the name from the ship manifest she'd seen on Rifflen. "Viktor?"

"Lucien. I'm the more handsome brother," Lucien corrected. He gave her a friendly smile. His eyes sparkled with flirtatious mischief. They were a curious mix of red and brown. "Trying to make a call?"

Violette didn't bother to deny what she'd been caught doing. "That's a pretty effectual way to keep people from using your equipment. Don't suppose you'd want to dial for me?"

Lucien laughed. "Rick said you were witty."

"I don't know if I'd take Rick's opinion on anything," Violette replied.

"He also says you're the one who is going to break Dev's curse." Lucien sat in his chair and smiled up at her. "So, are you fire? That's the obvious choice because of Dev. Wood and frost doesn't make sense. And metal is well, everyone is flying around in metal these days. Or are you earth because we first saw you on Rifflen under the sand?"

"Am I earth?" Violette arched a brow.

"The curse. Are you earth because of the sand?"

"Are you having some kind of episode? What exactly are you on?" She studied his eyes a little more carefully. Maybe they weren't normal for his type of humanoid. "Have you been drinking Torganian rum? You do know that isn't really liquor and causes hallucinations in most humanoids, don't you? If you partook, we need to get you into a medical booth."

"Oh, trust me, I know all about Torganian *roome-ah*. We found out that lesson the hard way when we accidentally kidnapped a cat prince and tried to, anyway, that's a long story. Prince Falke is fine now and back with his people. Point being, I don't touch the stuff."

"Then, you actually want to know if I'm made of earth?" Violette arched a brow.

Lucien tilted his head. "Dev did tell you he's cursed, didn't he?"

"Cursed," she repeated.

"Yeah, cursed. Like honest to whiteholes, predicted by a dead seer, cursed."

"I don't believe in superstitions. Dev isn't cursed because he has Bevlon blood. It's just blood, a collection of genetic anomalies prevalent in his people more than other alien races and..." Violette's voice tapered off, and she realized she sounded like one of her father's speeches.

"That's all probably true, starlight, but I'm talking about an actual Lintianese spirit curse. Five of our crewmen have fallen victim to it. Five men will find or not find love according to the five Lintianese elements. Well, not Evan, his curse was broken by..." Lucien glanced away and pretended to adjust a couple of dials.

"By Josselyn," Violette filled in, frowning. If Josselyn somehow fit into their superstitious belief system that could explain why they were so protective of the newest member of their crew, and would fight so hard to defend her.

Lucien nodded. "Anyway, rumor has it you're breaking Dev's curse."

"And you believe I represent one of the five elements?" Violette chuckled. "I appreciate you think I'm some special spell breaker, but I'm not the end to anyone's curse."

"Oh, well, that's too bad. I hear Dev likes you."

Lucien shrugged and began flipping through his dials in earnest, scanning signal channels.

Dev often looked so stoic and serious. She assumed he liked her, at least well enough to take her as a lover, but to hear it from one of his friends filled her with pleasure.

"Where do I find food?" she asked.

Lucien pointed in the direction of the dining area.

Violette bowed her head by way of a valediction and left communications to seek out the dining hall. Once alone in the passageway, she smiled to herself. It was a romantic notion, thinking she was Dev's true love come to end a curse. She envied those who could find such happiness in life.

She moved down the corridor listening for voices, but the ship was quiet. Her fingers traced the wall as she walked, absently gliding over the seams in the metal. In love with Dev? What an extraordinary idea. She never allowed herself to consider falling in love.

The mechanical hum of a door sliding open interrupted her thoughts and caused her to stop walking.

"I'll only be a moment. Everyone is asleep. I won't be—"

"Josselyn." Violette gasped, the sound causing

the woman to stop speaking. Dev had lied. Her sister was on board the ship.

Josselyn turned. Her mouth slightly agape, she whispered, "Violette."

For a long time, she could only stare. Her hands shook, and her mind became paralyzed. She'd waited for this moment when she would have the woman before her, only now she wasn't prepared. None of the words she'd wanted to say came to mind. Every speech, every sentence was lost.

Violette screamed incoherently, charging forward. Josselyn shrieked in surprise and made a move to jump out of the way. Violette grabbed the woman's hair. She jerked her arm back, and someone caught her wrist before she could strike.

Violette recognized Dev's heated touch before she saw his face. He dragged her away from Josselyn. When they stopped moving, she watched Evan stand before his wife like a shield.

"You…killed," Violette managed. All the building anger and grief flowed through her until she shook. She wanted to scream, to hit. Tears ran down her cheeks. "You…killed…"

"Violette." Josselyn's tone was pitying. The sound only made the pain worse. Violette didn't want Josselyn's pity. "Please, don't do this. We're sisters."

"You're not my sister," Violette denied.

Dev kept a hold on her arms, and she tried to pull free of his grasp.

"Come away," he whispered. "We'll talk."

"I don't want to talk to you," Violette countered. "You led me to believe she wasn't on this ship."

"Actually, I told you that," Lochlann stated. He joined them, looking as if the noise had just woken him from a deep sleep. "It was a decision made for the safety of all on board. However, now that you know, I don't think we have any choice but to lock you up. Dev, will you bring her to a holding area? Or should I have Jackson?"

"That won't be necessary," Dev stated.

"No, please, don't do that," Josselyn inserted. "I'll stay away from her. Don't lock her up."

"Don't try to help me," Violette snapped. "You're not my sister. You're a murderer."

"Please, Lochlann, let Dev take her to the medical booth." Josselyn lifted her hands to show she wasn't going to show aggression. She tried to step around her husband. "I have an idea."

"What do you have in mind?" Evan asked, not making it easy for her to pass.

"Genetic testing will prove we're sisters. Maybe then she'll—" Josselyn tried to answer.

"That won't change anything," Violette interrupted. "The fact we shared a mother does not make you my sister. I listened to the holo-boxes. I know you were engaged to my father when he was younger. You perpetrated some crime and were put into stone, and he grew up. He married your mother, not you, and they had me out of their love. He saved her. He was a good man. Out of loyalty he had you pardoned and the second you were free you committed murder. He should have left you there to rot."

"Do you even know what you're saying? Do you just rewrite history to suit your storyline?" Josselyn cried in frustration. She pushed her husband forcibly out of her way. "I have given you evidence, words out of Jack's mouth in holographic form. It should be enough to open your mind to the possibility that more happened than what you've been told by your father. For one, I was never engaged to him. He asked. I said no. He didn't like that. So he betrayed his people by helping the government on the planet of Florencia spy on us. They wanted to take over the individual moons. They wanted power over us, our land, and our money. The second the Federation showed up offering to help, Jack was right there with his hand out greedy for their shiny promises and pretty words."

"I don't rewrite history," Violette denied. She breathed hard. "I saw my father killed by your hand. That's what I know."

"And I saw my whole world fall by the hand of

your father," Josselyn countered. "My brothers, they would have been your half-brothers, and my father were murdered. Let me give you a little history lesson, sis. When Florencia couldn't deliver the moons to the Federation, they killed the head of the Florencian planet government and laid claim to the lands with some sham treaty clause before turning their forces to the moon. Again, there was colony spy Jack, all ready to kill whoever they told him to for his shiny white uniform and sparkly title. He proved he was a good little Federation lapdog by storming into my village and slaughtering nearly everyone. Those who weren't killed were put into stone prisons. They destroyed everything I love. And when it looked as if we might win, they destroyed the weather satellites. They killed all life on those moons and then abandoned them to ice. When it was all said in done, they had killed colonies of people for a few forced recruits to fight in their armies and…" Josselyn's voice caught. "And…"

Violette saw the woman's expression. Josselyn believed what she said. The pain in it mirrored her own.

"Josselyn," Evan urged softly, pulling her toward him. "It will be all right, baby."

Violette didn't know what to believe anymore. She watched Dev out of the corner of her eye, wishing he'd pull her close and whisper soothingly to her. Instead, he kept a firm hold on her as if to keep her from attacking.

"I understand your pain, but if you're going to kill for something, don't you want to know if it's for the truth?" Josselyn reached a hand forward as if she'd touch her.

Violette jerked. Dev's grip restrained her. "Let me go." She jerked again. "Dev, let me go!"

Dev released her. Violette pushed past him, moving away from Josselyn and the others. She ran down the corridor. There was nowhere to go. The ship might have been bigger than hers, but it still felt small. She heard footsteps behind her and paused, glancing around. Dev caught up with her.

"Dev, I," she took several deep breaths, "Dev, I…"

"Come." He gently touched her elbow and led her into a room. Dev's shirt lay across the narrow mattress. It was then she looked more fully at him. He wore only pants. His chest and feet were bare.

"Dev, I…"

"I thought it best for you to learn the truth before you saw your sister," Dev said. "I never meant to deceive you. I regret letting you believe a lie, but—"

"Dev, don't take this away from me," she whispered. Tears burned her eyes. "Revenge is all I have."

"No, you are more than revenge," he said.

"No. That's all I have left." Violette gestured helplessly, unsure what she should do next. She wasn't used to feeling vulnerable. "I have no family. I have a crew who like me well enough, but if I stopped paying them, they'd leave me without a backward glance. I owe it to my father. I made a blood oath the day he died to get justice. It is who I am. I need it."

"Violette, you have me," Dev whispered. "If you want me."

Violette wished that was true. She wanted the words she read into his comment were real. She wanted to hear him say he loved her, needed her, chose her.

Though, what would happen if he had to choose? Her or Josselyn? His lover or a part of his crew? She didn't doubt he liked her, but how far would he go for like? She didn't want to hear the answer so didn't ask.

"Let me take you to Florencia's Fifth Moon so you can see for yourself," he said. "If your oath is for justice, then learn the truth and then decide what is just."

His words made sense. Instead of answering, she kissed him. Even if it wasn't love, she needed to feel his affection. She didn't want to be alone. It was only when he touched her could she pretend that the universe wasn't there.

Dev made love to her slowly, taking his time. First, he stripped her of her clothing. His hands moved over her legs, massaging their way up her thighs, her hips, her waist and back. She swayed on her feet, almost unable to stand. He caught her against his chest and lifted her gently from the floor to lay her on the bed.

He pushed the pants from his hips. Heat cocooned her when he brought his naked body over hers. The texture of his skin felt fantastic against hers. Her legs restlessly moved along his. She leaned up for a kiss, moaning as her moist tongue met his.

When he entered her, it was slow and steady. Her eyes connected with his. The full length of him filled her. She wanted the moment to last. Every nerve focused on him. He rocked against her, staying deep. The pleasure came almost too soon before she was ready to let the moment go. Their climax crashed against them in trembling perfection. Finally, her eyes closed, as she was unable to resist the lull of ecstasy.

Afterward, Dev held her against him on the small bed. Even though there was a larger room waiting for her, she didn't want to leave his side.

"I don't think I can kill her. I thought I could,

but…" Violette turned in Dev's arms to look at him. "What kind of daughter does that make me?"

Dev didn't answer. He stroked her hair away from her face.

"You never mentioned that you're cursed by a spirit." She traced the red line on his skin. "Should I be worried?"

"More like tormented by one. Zhang An gave a vague prophecy that is open to interpretation. The idea was meant to worm its way into our heads to plague us." He skimmed his fingers down her arm and back up again.

"What was the prophecy?"

"It was for Rick, Lochlann, Jackson, Evan and me. She said something along the line of, we'd find our love hidden within the mystery of the five elements of the Lintianese people—water, fire, wood, earth, and metal. One element for each of us. Our assigned element will hold the secret to our future happiness. But, since she didn't tell us which element was ours, we have no idea what we're looking for. Apparently, if we don't recognize our fate, we'll be cursed to living our lives alone. How did you hear about the curse?"

"Lucien in communications."

Dev chuckled. "I should have known you would try to go to communications."

"So does the curse plague you?" Violette

continued to trace the lines on his chest. "Are you looking?"

"Sadly, yes. It is hard not to contemplate the idea that my future happiness hinges on signs that I must see. The danger is, when you're looking, it's possible to see signs in everything."

"I think you're metal." Violette pressed her hand flat against his chest. "Because you have a hard shell like the hull of a ship and you have a stubborn personality."

"Rick thinks I'm fire because I'm Bevlon, and they first met me when I was about to be set on fire by heretics."

"No, that's too obvious." Violette shook her head in denial. She ran her hand down between them to the unyielding length growing between his thighs. "I definitely think you're metal. Molten, red hot steel."

"And are you trying to break my curse?" he asked, angling so that he lay completely on his back to give her access to his body.

"Oh, fireballs, no." She leaned over and kissed him as she crawled to straddle his waist. The heat of his stomach hit her sex, instantly moistening it. She winked teasingly at him and slid back until her ass was against his arousal. "I don't believe in curses and predetermined fates. I believe we make our own happiness and destiny."

"And, right now, with me, are you happy?" he asked.

"Yes." The honestly of the answer surprised her. "Right now, with you, I'm very happy, Dev."

He growled and pulled her down for his kiss. No more words were needed, but then neither one of them had been incredibly forthcoming about expressing themselves with conversation. They spoke a much more primitive language, one that didn't need words to be understood.

CHAPTER 20

Ice Complex Five, Florencia's Fifth Moon, Four days later...

Stepping out onto the surface of Florencia's Fifth Moon was like climbing inside a biofreeze container in her underwear. The two-piece snowsuit offered protection, but even that wasn't enough to stop the cold from creeping into her fingers and toes. Dev had given her the thick, black clothing to wear. It matched the others, except for Jackson who was in white. She doubted they'd come by the Federation snowsuits honestly. The fact they still had patches on them proved they were not decommissioned uniforms.

Jackson's white suit had the ESC emblem for the Exploratory Science Commission, as did the skintight jumpsuits they wore underneath. Thinking of it, she glanced at Dev. The elastic material had stretched to fit him, molding to his body to hide his flesh while showing every sexy detail of his frame. She could still picture the firm look of his ass in tight black without even closing her eyes.

"How are you?" Dev asked.

"Unconcerned." She took a deep breath. The cold stung her cheeks and nose. "I'm not worried about what we're going to find here. I have every confidence that what you think is going to be disproven by what we see here."

It was a lie. She wasn't confident of that fact. Doubts had started to creep into her thoughts ever since Josselyn had her say about family history.

Besides Dev and Jackson, Rick, Lucien, Viktor, Evan and Josselyn also joined them on the planet's surface. Lochlann stayed on the ship where he could monitor them from the sky. The craft hovered in orbit after dropping them off.

"I can see why they chose this place," Violette said. The moon revolved around an uninhabited planet. At one time it looked as if it had been culti-vated to support life, but that would have been a long time ago. Now ice had claimed the surface. "It makes for a perfect prison. Isolated. They would be able to see unauthorized ships coming before they even flew into orbit. If anyone escaped, they wouldn't survive long on the surface."

Jackson gave a humorless laugh. "I don't think escape is what they were concerned about."

"No, they only cared about hiding what they had done," Rick muttered.

"If we find proof of who is responsible, we'll make sure it's known," Lucien said. "Secrets have a way of coming out eventually."

"Be careful, some people don't want their secrets known." Violette saw the way that the crew looked at her. She was the outsider to be watched, tied to the evil Federation boogeyman.

Her gaze moved toward Josselyn. The sisters hadn't spoken since the incident in the spaceship corridor. Even though Violette stopped saying she wanted to kill her sister that didn't mean she'd given up on bringing her father's killer to justice. She had to know the truth and then she would decide what justice meant.

For the women's safety, the men had decided to keep the sisters separated as much as they could. On the ship, it had proven to be easy. Violette preferred spending her time in Dev's tiny room to mingling with the crew. Now, they kept them apart by putting two crewmen between the sisters at all times. For a moment, her gaze locked with Josselyn's. Evan leaned to his wife and whispered. Josselyn nodded and looked away first.

Violette shivered and found herself gravitating

toward the heat of Dev's body. The cloudless blue-gray sky seemed as dead as the frozen earth. When he glanced down in surprise at her sudden affection, she muttered, "I hate the cold."

He lifted his arm around her shoulders and drew her closer.

Quietly, so the others couldn't hear, she asked, "How are you doing with the temperatures? The cold is not hurting you is it?"

"I'm fine as long as I stay in the suit." Dev showed her the device on his wrist. "Viktor rigged it so I can monitor my temperature."

"You'll say something if it becomes dangerous?" she insisted. "I remember what you told me about Bevlons and the cold."

He nodded.

Violette needed to be here, to see the truth for herself—whatever truth there was left to see. But, that didn't mean she *wanted* to be here. She wanted to be a child again, feeling trapped by the sands churning outside the windows for the military base, before her father gave her a scar and started this mystery she'd been tormented by.

"Someone blasted a hole in the weather shuttle. We saw it the first time we landed," Rick said. "Whoever it was wanted this moon to stop thriving. It probably froze over in less than a day."

Josselyn had said as much.

"If you need proof, we can fly past it once we get back to the ship," Rick added.

"It was so beautiful here," Josselyn said, more to Evan than to anyone else, but Violette heard her clearly. They each puffed white breaths of air. Maneuvering over icy terrain wasn't easy, but she doubted that is what caused the pained look on Josselyn's face. The woman continued, "On clear nights you could see the weather shuttles moving over the skies. There was a control room where we could modify the weather schedule, but it was best to let the seasons run their cycle. Though, I remember my father making it rain for my mother one warm night. I watched them dance from a window."

Violette said nothing. It was hard to think of her mother's first marriage, of a life she was never allowed to have, of moments and memories. Her mother was an idea, a holographic picture, a story told—and possibly fabricated—by her father. Josselyn's mother was a dance in the rain, a series of gestures and movements available to reminiscence upon at will.

Violette tried to ball her hand into a fist, but the gloves made it difficult. Josselyn had the life a daughter should have. She had a husband who adored her, friends who would give their lives to protect her, and a past of love to draw from.

Violette was jealous, and she hated that about herself. The general had loved her, but he was a busy man, always off on some mission doing alientarian work. Violette looked at Dev. His arms tightened around her. Even her own lover was on Josselyn's side. The whole reason she was here was because Dev wanted her to stop hunting her sister.

"The first days of summer were so brilliant when the sun was closest to the shuttle, and we could feel the magnified heat." Josselyn shivered, rubbing her hands along her arms to generate warmth. "And now, look at it."

Violette pulled out of Dev's embrace with the excuse of navigating the arctic trail. She did look. Time had frozen on the icy surface creating sculptures of the past, preserving it like some dead curiosity. Crop rows were organized over the gentle slope of the outlying landscape. An orchard stretched into the distance, the many limbs contrasting the lighter sky like shiny black fingers. The crew followed a trail of footprints along the field's edge. She had the feeling of walking through her sister's memory, a place where time had stopped.

"Take away the ice and everything is how I remember it." Josselyn turned her attention to the prison complex. "Except for that."

The metal building was out of place on the

small moon. The sharp corners of the structure were in typical military fashion, and it sat in a spot of convenience with no thought to the surrounding aesthetics. A prison was for function, not beauty.

Violette felt a hand on her shoulder. She knew it was Dev without looking. He wanted to continue to comfort her, but she couldn't allow it. Already she was nervous about what this place would reveal. It was taking all of her energy to remain strong.

"It doesn't look as if anyone has visited since we were last here," Dev said. "The compound should be easy to unlock."

Though it was an older style discontinued a hundred years ago, Violette knew the basic layout of the prison before entering. The metal walls kept out the snow but not the cold. Sensors kicked on at their presence, and the biocell still provided enough power to light the hallways and switch on the facility computer monitors.

Rick led the way with Jackson, quickly stepping as if he wished to hurry through this part of his mission.

"Grab anything of value," Jackson ordered. "This will be the last time we come here."

Dev strode alongside Violette, not touching her again. Lucien and Viktor whispered amongst themselves. It sounded like they bickered, but she couldn't hear what their argument was about.

"We should wait here in the hall," Evan said to his wife. "I don't want you to see them."

Josselyn evidently didn't listen as their footsteps continued to follow into the large prison hold in the center of the compound. The open room served as a staging area for those locked in stone. Lucien and Viktor took off to explore the far rooms for valuables.

The first statue prisoner wasn't what Violette expected to see. The Federation's official images of the failed immobile prisoner project had shown men with bound hands standing dignified in a red stone-like state. Their expressions were serene and their posture relaxed. The Ice Complex prisoners were terrified. Arms rose eternally to hide faces as if that gesture could have saved them from this fate. After being imprisoned, they'd been murdered in their defenseless states. Their body parts had been broken off. Skulls had been crushed. Stone limbs were thrown into piles. Violette walked past a woman's head. Every detail of her screaming mouth could be seen. Another man was locked in what looked to be prayer, or perhaps he was begging his captors for mercy.

"The perfect prisoners," Rick stated with a sarcastic drawl. "They don't sleep, don't eat, don't piss, don't beg for mercy."

"Bastards," Lucien swore, having heard Rick's

comment as he came out room only to disappear into another one.

"No one deserves this," Jackson agreed.

"It shouldn't be like this," Violette said. There were, at least, a couple dozen prisoners, maybe more. None of them were dressed in prison-issued suits. They were in gowns and tunic shirts. Even their hair wasn't the standard prisoner cut from a hundred years ago. She had hoped that there might be a way to free whoever was left here. They'd thawed Josselyn from her prison, and Violette could get her hands on more medicine to reverse the effects of an imperfect freezing process. But, there was no saving the people here. If the prisoners were thawed from their stone state, they would instantly die from their injuries.

Violette pulled the dark cap from her head to expose her ears and head. She breathed hard, looking at the red dust coating the floor. They stepped on bits of the statue. Footprints marred the dust, presumably from when the crew had visited the prison the first time.

"No, no, no," Josselyn whispered, rushing past Violette to go to a small boy on the floor. He couldn't have been more than thirteen years. Long hair hung over his eyes. "I know him. This is Tyson. He played with my brother. They put him in stone and then shot him as if he were some target for practice. There are laser marks on his chest. He…" Josselyn turned and pointed to a woman close by. "And that's his mother. Murielle worked in my home in the kitchens. She didn't do anything to anyone. She…"

Violette inched away as Josselyn's grief built. There was nothing that could be done.

"Do you see?" Josselyn demanded, turning to find Violette. "This is why I had to…"

This was not what Violette expected to find. Yes, what happened here was horrible, but that didn't mean her father did it. He had tried to rescue Josselyn. The holo-box proved that. He pardoned her. He tried to get her out.

"I know all of them," Josselyn told Evan, crying. He murmured something comforting to her.

"These rooms are clear," Lucien announced as they rejoined the group.

Violette had to get away from the misery in Josselyn's voice. She followed the old footsteps on the floor, assuming they would lead her to what she needed to see next.

"There is no honor in this," Jackson approached Josselyn. His tone was flat, almost militant in its clipped tone. "And nothing we can do to change events. We will honor them by telling their story."

"Jackson is right," Lucien said.

"We're prepared to scavenge for the truth this time," Viktor added.

"Medical laboratory is this way." Rick brushed past Violette. "It's where we found the lot numbers for the prisoners on a hand-held. We couldn't assess the computer because we didn't have the code, but we're hoping you'll have more luck being as you're Federation."

"I'm not Federation," Violette denied.

"Close enough, starshine," Rick answered. The endearment didn't sound very pleasant. She found herself almost wishing he'd call her Velvet Violette again, or some such ridiculous nickname.

"I'll bring up the screen," Lucien said, moving to the system console in the medical laboratory. "I don't have the codes to do much else."

Violette stared at the floating screen as it appeared over the computer console. Lucien stepped out of her way. All portable equipment had been cleared from the room, as was protocol when decommissioning a facility, but since the computer was wired into the main complex, it remained intact.

She slowly sat before the console and contemplated what she should do. Lying was always an option, but then she'd come for the truth. It was the only way she could decide what path to take. She closed her eyes, trying to remember how to calculate the code to unlock the device.

"Can you open it or not?" Jackson asked.

"I can't concentrate with everyone staring at me," Violette snapped. She gave him a hard look.

"Wait outside," Dev ordered the others.

With some reluctance, they agreed.

"Thank you," Violette said. "I promised you I'd seek the truth, but I can't think with all of them staring at me like I'm the gatekeeper of all things evil."

"They don't think that." Dev leaned against the counter. "They believe you to be an honorable person."

Violette arched a brow.

"Misguided, but honorable," Dev amended. He ran the backs of his fingers over her cheek. "And beautiful."

"I doubt beauty enters into the equation." She leaned into his hand. "How are you still warm?"

"Your face is almost as red as mine. Put your hat back on." He handed the cap to her. She didn't remember dropping it. Taking it, she slid it over her head. It was warm from his hold.

Violette wasn't military, but since her father was a general he'd taught her how to access basic military files. Anything too highly encrypted would have needed bio-signatures of some kind.

It took a moment, but she was able to figure out a basic password that allowed her mid-level access. "It's not much, just facility maintenance records. Since the prisoners were in stone, there were no feeding schedules, exercise hours, or anything else to note. I can get you some names, but no crimes. There is an old incident report for a couple of the guards who had an argument that ended in punches. Most of it is inventory supplies and requisition requests. I'm sorry. I know you wanted something fantastic to expose this place, but there's…" Violette paused as she scrolled through the work orders and memos to the earliest ones. The first file had her father's military identification number on it. "My father."

"What does it say?" Dev leaned over to look at the holographic screen. She felt his heat against her neck. She turned to him, seeing his cheek near her lips.

"It's a personnel file." Violette didn't open it.

Dev looked at her. His mouth was close to hers. She felt his breath on her lips. The warm caress was intimate, and she breathed him inside of her.

"Open it," he said. "You're here for the truth."

She nodded and turned to the screen. The file had a picture of her father as a young man. He looked different out of uniform. His clothes matched those of the broken prisoners. The image turned, showing first his front and then a profile view of his upper body.

"Jack Stephans, Florencia Moon Coalition lead informant for sector five, status active, trusted," Violette read. She scrolled down the file, coming to a later entry. "Recommended for a high honor for his role in securing the Fifth Moon, as well as his work in subduing the rebel leaders hiding there. All rebellion has been terminated. Promotion: Ice Complex Five Warden. New file, classified." She frowned. "He never told me he was a warden."

That would mean the general did know what happened here, at least enough of it. It also meant Josselyn had told the truth. *Jack Stephans, Florencia Moon Coalition lead informant for sector five.* He was the Federation's inside man to what had happened here. Why else would they have promoted a mere local spy to warden so quickly unless he proved in some great way he could be trusted? She thought about the broken statues, posed in fear. Her father was a monster.

"I don't think he was the warden when the statues were broken," Dev said, as if that would be a comfort.

Violette's heartbeat quickened, and she tried to keep her composure.

Rick appeared at the door. "Anything?"

Dev shook his head in denial. "She's in, but there's nothing useful."

"I'll copy it anyway for Lucien to go through." Jackson pushed past Rick and withdrew an information transfer disc from his snowsuit. He laid it on the computer mainframe. The holographic screen appeared to be sucked into the disc before returning to normal. Jackson slid the disc back into his pocket. "Temperature is dropping outside. We need to leave if we're going to scavenge what we can from the castle. Josselyn knows where all the real treasure is hidden. If you're done here, let's get moving. I don't want to become another one of this moon's human icicles."

CHAPTER 21

"Holy space balls, I forgot how cold this place was," Rick said, falling into stride next to Dev.

"I can't feel my space balls," Lucien complained, holding his lower stomach.

"That's cause you don't have any balls," Viktor answered.

"More balls than you do," Lucien argued.

"I'll show you how big my—" Viktor retorted.

"I will slap you both," Dev said calmly. The brothers stopped fighting and gave Dev a sheepish look, which he in turn ignored. Dev looked at the indicator on his wrist. "It wasn't this cold last time we were here." Touching Violette's arm to get her attention, he inquired, "Are you doing all right? You're not too cold?"

"My balls are fine, thank you," Violette

answered with a smirk. Lucien and Viktor snorted with laughter. Before Dev could say anything, she quickly amended, "I'm good. Let's just keep moving."

Dev thought about joking back but didn't want to encourage the brothers. Usually, he'd be worried about Rick, but there was something about this place that made the pilot unusually somber.

Dev admired Violette's strength. The last four days spent with her in his bed had been as close to perfection as any man could hope for. Attraction wasn't the problem. It was everything else in their lives weighing down on them.

"It's strange, right? Nothing has changed since we've been here. I mean, look, those are our footsteps," Lucien pointed at the ground, "and there is where Josselyn's feet dragged as we brought her back to the ship." He gave a short laugh. "Sorry about that. We didn't intend to almost drop you."

Josselyn paused to look at where he indicated. Dev knew this journey was painful for the woman. It had to be. They had all seen the torment she'd gone through after they freed her. He wished there was a way to show that anguish to Violette so that she might understand. Then again, he wished there was a way to show Josselyn how much Violette was hurting after the death of her father. Violette was like him in the sense they both hid their emotions from others. Perhaps that is why he understood her better than most. Or perhaps she'd let her guard down just enough when they were alone to allow him to peek inside.

The homestead had been built in a style far removed from Federation standards. A security wall circled the inner village and medieval castle. Jackson led the group through the main gate. Evan and Josselyn huddled together as they followed closely behind Jackson. Rick had cut the rusted metal lock on their first visit so getting inside was much more efficient this time around. A trail of prints led them under a second lower wall's arch. Dark spires and round towers were built into the walls, with walkways along the top sections.

"Look at those plants," Violette pointed out. Dev nodded. Grass shard stuck up from the ground like shiny narrow blades. "And those homes."

"They're called cottages," Josselyn answered, not turning to look back at her sister. "Our mother was the reigning lady, and she knew all the people who lived in the village. She would visit the cottages and make sure the people had everything they needed. She loved children and celebrated every new village birth. No one had a bad word to say about her. Everyone loved her. She was a true lady in body and spirit—delicate, charitable, kind, sheltered."

Dev watched Violette's face carefully. He saw the eagerness she tried to hide. When she looked around the village, it was as if her eyes couldn't take in what she was seeing before moving to the next object. She had no memory of her mother, and this was the closest she would ever come.

"Ignore the cottages and outbuildings," Josselyn said when Viktor began to stray off course. "Everything you'll want to salvage will be inside the castle."

Violette stopped walking and looked up. Gentle white puffs of air left her parted lips. The frozen castle loomed over the surrounding village. A sheen of ice preserved the stone beneath.

"Why were you held prisoner out here?" Violette asked. "It makes no sense as to why they'd—"

"Shh," Rick commanded. He raised his hand. Everyone turned their attention toward him. He lifted a life sign scanner they had acquired from a "technically" abandoned, locked, hidden ESC cargo crate on a remote planet. Jackson walked over to the pilot to look at the device. Rick scanned for life-forms in the distance.

Dev stepped protectively closer to Violette. Very quietly, he said, "They imprisoned Josselyn in one of the towers. She was too heavy to move, so they left her. That fact probably saved her life. When the other prisoners were broken, she was left unharmed." He pointed to the tallest tower where they'd found her. "She was up there."

Rick hit the device several times. "False alarm. It's not picking up anything now. The temperature must be causing it to glitch."

"Atmospheric reading still normal," Dev said. "But the temperature has dropped a few degrees. Let's keep moving."

As they neared the castle's front door, he detected the crushed area where Lucien and Viktor had gotten into a fight next to the sad frozen remains of some small hairy creature. He braced his weight against the door and pushed hard, bouncing his shoulder until the ice seam gluing it shut broke free.

"Let's get to work. Comms stay on," Dev ordered. Jackson had given him the lead on this part of the mission since he'd be with Josselyn and Violette the whole time and needed the authority to make judgment calls for the group if anything when wrong. "Stay in pairs and follow the maps Josselyn drew for you. Try to find the personal items she requested, otherwise, take the most valuable and transportable. Check in at each stop. Expandable crates are in your packs. Don't load them too heavy. We still have to drag them down to meet the ship if it's too cold for the hover attachments to work."

A soft light came through narrow windows from

outside to illuminate the entryway. When everyone had entered, Dev pushed the door closed.

Rick turned on the castle power. Flickering light flooded the inside from torch-shaped fixtures on the walls. "You heard the man, let's get to work."

Lucien and Viktor took off in one direction. Jackson and Rick went in another.

"I don't suppose we can find me a girlfriend this time," Lucien's soft voice came through the comms as they walked away. "Statue girl turned out all right for Evan."

"Sure, rocket boy, we can try defrosting that dog-creature outside. I think you might have a chance with it," Viktor answered.

"I'm not listening to this," Jackson's voice interrupted. "Dev, please, can we leave com-links on, but not open?"

"Fine," Dev stated. "Turn off the open channel, but leave them on. Be careful. It might look sturdy, but there is no telling the damage weather and time have done to this structure, especially in the timber-enforced sections. If you get your asses trapped under rubble, I might not dig them out."

CHAPTER 22

"I WANT TO SHOW YOU SOMETHING." Josselyn nodded that Violette should follow her. The groups had split up to explore the castle, but Dev and Evan kept the sisters together. Violette knew what they were trying to do. It was clear Evan wanted them to bond, and Dev wanted to make sure she didn't try to attack Josselyn. As an independent woman, babysitters annoyed her, but then, she had threatened to kill her sister on several occasions, so their concern was probably warranted.

Strange personal items filled the abandoned castle, and decorations hung as they had for over a hundred years. Time had stopped in this place, and Violette again had the feeling she was trespassing in someone else's memory. Josselyn led the group to a large dining hall. Tables were lined up in even rows on the stone floor. Dinnerware was set out as if a meal had been interrupted. Whatever food would have been on them looked long disintegrated. Josselyn took a couple of the plates and goblets and handed them to her husband. Evan pulled out an oversized expandable crate and put the items inside. She noticed carvings that reminded her of the wooden door to her father's office.

A cylinder fireplace was in the middle of the room. Violette would have loved to start it. Maybe then feeling would come back to her fingertips. There were more torch fixtures to light the way. Banners covered parts of the walls in large woven strips.

"That tapestry," Josselyn told Evan. The large cloth had men and animals sewn onto it. The men lifted swords over their heads in battle. "It was my father's favorite. Try to be careful with it. I can't believe the material lasted in this weather."

Dev moved to help Evan retrieve the tapestry. Josselyn tossed a few small items in the crate. They made clanking noises as they landed against the side of the container.

Violette stood very still and didn't touch anything. What right did she have to these things? Her father had left this property to Josselyn. The day he gave her the scar, he'd told her, *"The land I spoke of does not belong to you. You will never see it. You would not want it."*

This land, this strange fairytale countryside covered in ice, and the castle in the center of it all, was not hers. The general had never wanted her to see it. Or was it he never wanted her to learn the truth of what it represented? If she hadn't found that holo-box as a child, would he have ever told her that Josselyn existed? It seemed rather obvious now that secrets had been buried here. She knew the Federation's ways well enough to know this was not how things were normally done. Her father was very wrong about one thing. Violette did want this. She wanted everything this place represented, everything she had not had in childhood.

"What did you want to show me?" Violette asked.

"Over here." Josselyn crossed the room to the far side. She stopped and looked up at a banner and said, "the Craven family crest," before reading the inscribed words, "*Ago pugna quod intereo per veneration.*"

"I've seen it," Violette answered somewhat defensively. It was one of the few things she had known about this place. "Honor above all else."

"Live, fight, and die with honor," Josselyn corrected, before she pointed at a large portrait. "That's our mother."

The likeness of a beautiful woman stared out

over the hall. The paint was dull and faded, but that did not take away from the sereneness of her expression. Her dark brown hair was pulled to the top of her head, immaculately placed. The square neckline of her gown showcased a jeweled necklace. The dress had two parts to it. The red overtunic was edged with cream lace. The full sleeves only hung to the elbows. The younger version of their mother looked like Josselyn, especially around the eyes.

"She smelled like honey with a hint of lavender," Josselyn said. "She was a good, gentle woman with a heart big enough for the whole galaxy. We protected her from the rebellion's affairs. She never knew Jack's part in it." Josselyn placed a hand on her sister's arm and drew Violette's attention to her. "When I almost died from the thawing process, or died and came back, whatever you'd like to call what happened after you saw me in the general's office, I had a vision of my family. They were here, in this room. In the vision, my mother told me about you. I don't know what you believe happens when we die, but I know I will come back here and be with my family."

Violette's gaze traveled a few feet to the next portrait. Her mother was there with her first husband, a very young Josselyn, and four boys. The children were grinning and mischievous while the parents gazed lovingly at each other.

"What are their names?" Violette studied the boys who would have been her half-brothers.

"Jonathan, Peter, Ralphe, and Rainier," Josselyn replied. "They died the day I was imprisoned, as did my father, Lord Craven."

"She's beautiful and so young." Violette stared up at their mother. "I saw holographic images of her, but she didn't look like that." She looked down to study her cold hands. "Your mother doesn't have the hollowness in her expression that mine did."

"She is our mother——" Josselyn began.

"No." Violette turned her eyes back up. "That woman did not have me. My mother was some shell of that woman. If given a choice, Lady Craven would never have become pregnant with me. Because if I accept what my father did here, then I have to admit that I was a mistake. He tricked our mother into marrying him and into having me."

"No, she wasn't like that," Josselyn protested. "She loved all her children. I'm sure that hollowness that you're describing was the loss she felt after losing so many of us."

And when it came to me, she couldn't be a parent again, so she chose death, Violette thought.

"In my vision she told me of you," Josselyn continued. "She said you were a good soul, troubled but one who would find your way to us eventually. I know she regretted that she couldn't be the mother that she was to the rest of us. I know she loved you."

"It's a pleasant thought, but I don't believe in that kind of afterlife. When I die, there will be no reason for my spirit to be transported here." Violette placed her hand over her long scar. The padding of the snowsuit kept her from feeling it. Somehow, looking at the happiness of Josselyn's family, the world they had lived in, the love shining in their faces, she had no more doubts. "I've tried so hard to believe what I've been told my entire life, but none of the holographic photos I've seen of my parents showed her looking at my father like that. She did not love my father. I shouldn't have been born. None of this should have happened. Whatever the Federation wanted with this place was so unimportant they let it all die. And my father? Why else would a general in the Federation try so hard to prove he was a good man unless he was desperately attempting to atone for something?"

"I just wanted you to see her, how she was, I didn't mean to make you feel—" Josselyn tried to explain.

"You should take those," Violette said, indicating the portraits. "I'd think you'd want to keep them."

Dev and Evan had put the tapestry into the crate and walked toward them. Hearing Violette's words, they automatically moved to grab the portraits.

"We're at the top of the tall tower," Lucien's voice came over the com-link. "Items located. Loading now."

"Good," Dev answered.

They heard footsteps nearby. Evan and Dev shared a look.

"I thought the others were searching the towers first and then working their way down," Josselyn said.

Dev reached for his com. "Jackson, Rick, check in." He paused, before repeating, "Jackson, Rick, check in."

There was no answer.

"Jackson, Rick, what the hell is going on?" Evan demanded into his com.

"What's happening?" Lucien's voice answered. "We can't hear their answer."

"Jackson, Rick, report in now," Dev commanded.

"Where do you—" Evan began.

"I don't think Jackson and Rick are up to talking at the moment," a harsh voice echoed from the doorway behind them. "They're indisposed, disposed, indisposed? I can never remember which is the right word."

"*Sacre*," Violette swore under her breath at the unexpected sound.

"*Sacrelue*," Josselyn whispered the antiquated version of the curse at the same time.

Gil nodded toward Violette in terse greeting. He lifted a small cylindrical device. Dev and Evan gasped in unison as the comms in their ears made electrical popping noises. The men instantly pulled the broken units away from their face and dropped them on the floor.

The Angelion's torn wing had been bound so only one slightly lifted as he came forward. He held a blaster pointed at them. Violette pushed in front of Dev, who in turn tried to grab her arm to pull her back behind him. She dodged his grasp.

"Gil, what are you doing here?" Violette lifted her hands to keep the others behind her as she dealt with her crewman.

"I could ask you the same thing," the man responded. "Doesn't exactly appear that you're here unwillingly."

"How did you know where to find us?" she asked.

"I placed a tracking device on their ship while it was docked on Quazer," Gil said. "We would have come for you sooner, but I was preoccupied with my medically induced coma."

"I assure you a rescue is not necessary. I need

you to let Jackson and Rick go," Violette commanded.

Gil kept his gun trained on them as he walked over to the crate. He reached inside and picked up a goblet. Angrily, he threw it. The cup clanged along the stone floor. "What in the space blasts is this crap? We come to liberate you only to find you shopping for home décor?"

"Who is here with you?" Violette demanded. Gil was clearly not in his right mind. If he were he'd have obeyed her order to stand down. "Jo wouldn't slither into this weather, so I'm guessing he's still on the ship. Ghost doesn't care enough to get his hands dirty. So that leaves Isaac."

"Isaac," Gil said conversationally. "You want to greet the captain?"

"I don't have a captain." Isaac entered the room behind Gil. "I thought I did, but she joined another crew while still owing us space credits."

"Then why are you here?" Violette felt Dev's hand on her shoulder. He tried to pull her gently back. She held her ground. "The last payment to the ship hasn't processed. You get paid when I get paid, same deal as always."

"I don't trust those in league with a Bevlon," Gil sneered. He pointed his gun directly at her. "His time is up. Move aside."

"You have to use a gun?" Dev laughed mockingly. "Trust an Angelion to be too scared for a real fight. Afraid I'll rip the other wing?"

"Dev, I don't think you're helping," Violette muttered between clenched teeth. She held her hand to her side, trying to gesture him back. "Gil, I get your age old family feud, but Isaac? You're better than this. Why take up Gil's cause? You know he's never going to return your feel—"

"You think I'm here because of Gil's feud with the Bevlon?" Isaac rubbed his blue forehead at the base of his horn. "You lost my loyalty the moment you abandoned your duty." He pointed at Josselyn. "There she is, Captain, kill her. Family honor demands it. That is still the plan, isn't it?"

"Things are more complicated," Violette said.

"No, they're not." Isaac trained his gun on Josselyn. "She killed your father. The details are just noise. You humans muddle everything with emotions. It's quite simple where I'm standing. If you can't avenge your father, then why would you feel loyalty to avenge your crew? Your breed of human cowardice cannot be trusted. At least, Gil carries on the fight of his people. I have nothing against the Bevlons, but I respect his loyalty to his people and in my loyalty to my crewman I'll help him as I was willing to help you."

"Don't you dare question my authority—" Violette began.

"You promised," Josselyn interrupted loudly.

Violette turned in surprise to look at her sister.

"You promised if I showed you where the jewels were you'd let my brothers go," Josselyn continued.

Violette arched a brow in confusion. She glanced up at the family picture. All of Josselyn's brothers were dead.

"Josselyn," Evan began.

"Jewels?" Isaac repeated. The interest in his voice was unmistakable. His gun arm relaxed some.

Violette saw the look on Josselyn's face and slowly nodded. She took several steps away Dev and the others. Her foot crunched Dev's discarded communicator on the floor. Hardening her tone, she said, "I told you it was complicated. I had this under control but since you space cadets are insisting on doing this the hard way…" She let her voice trail off as she moved to join Gil and Isaac. "Hand me a gun so we can finish this."

Gil eyed her suspiciously. "We'll keep the guns."

"You don't trust me? You saw the jewels she gave us to pay for her ride to Rifflen. We're talking an entire treasury full of the stuff. Why else would I come to this icehole of a settlement?" Violette pretended to be exasperated with them. In reality, she was terrified. Before she was just one of the guys, floating around space earning a living. Now she had something to lose—a sister, a man she loved. Why didn't she tell Dev she loved him? Seeing a gun pointed at them, knowing Jackson and Rick might already be dead, made their situation all the more terrifying. If it weren't for her, they wouldn't have been in this situation.

"Where are these jewels?" Isaac asked.

Good. Greed. Violette could work with greed.

"I'll show you," Dev said, making a move to go forward.

"Nice try, demon," Gil said. "Step back and out of the snowsuit."

"Gil, that isn't necessary," Violette said. "Lock them up. We'll keep them as leverage if Josselyn doesn't behave."

"You, too, out of the snowsuit," Gil ordered Evan. When the men didn't comply, he held the gun toward Violette's head. Her eyes met his, pleading with him not to obey. The temperatures were too low for him to survive long without protection. "Do it, or I kill her."

Dev glared and shrugged out of his snowsuit. When he stood in the skintight underclothes, he tossed the snowsuit toward Gil's feet. Evan did the same.

"Seems like the beast has a fondness for you," Isaac observed in distaste. "Wonder why that is?"

"Gil, you can't leave them like that. The cold temperatures will kill them," Violette said.

"One less Bevlon to worry about." He answered, unconcerned.

"Isaac, tie them." Gil motioned at Josselyn. "You come with us. Take us to the jewels."

"No," Josselyn said. "You let them go. Let the others go. Then I'll take you to the treasure. You can do whatever you want to me, but don't hurt anyone else."

Violette knew what Josselyn was trying to do, but it wouldn't work. Isaac produced laser shackles to bind Evan and Dev's wrists, and then anchored the ends into the stone floor, trapping both men in their places. Dev looked as if he wanted to tear the Corge man apart.

"We don't torture," Violette stated. "Give them back their suits."

"Treasure, now," Gil ordered Josselyn.

Violette dared a glance back as Josselyn led them from the old dining hall. Dev and Evan trembled violently without the protection of their suits. With the outside temperatures continuing to drop, Evan wouldn't last more than an hour, if that. She didn't want to think about how much faster the temperature would affect Dev.

"I'm sorry," Violette mouthed. He nodded once.

She turned to walk beside her crew. Gil dropped back. She knew he trained the gun on her back. She'd seen the look on his face. He thought she'd betrayed him. Perhaps she had. When she didn't let him kill Dev, when she took Dev to her bed and put Gil into a medically induced coma so she wouldn't have to deal with him, when she didn't fight harder to tell her crew what had happened to her, all those times she'd betrayed him.

As a Corge, Isaac's motivations were easy to comprehend. She lost his trust the moment she refused to kill Josselyn. It was that straightforward. His kind understood things in very simple terms.

Jo would be loyal to the ship, no matter who was in charge of it. *Racing Banana* was his baby. And Ghost, well, who knew what Ghost was thinking.

Violette didn't dare look at Josselyn. She hoped the woman knew what she was doing. Not that Violette had any better ideas. Playing to greed was an almost foolproof way of buying a little more time.

"What did you do to the others?" Violette asked, trying to sound unconcerned.

"Jackson and Rick won't be joining us," Isaac answered.

Josselyn made a faint noise. Violette tried to alter her course by small degrees to bring Gil into her peripheral. He stayed just out of her sight.

"The treasury is this way," Josselyn said. "The deal still stands, right? I show you, you don't harm my brothers?"

"Shut your black hole," Violette ordered. "No more delays."

Her aggressive display was probably too little too late. Gil and Isaac wouldn't trust her unless they saw her pull the trigger on her sister.

Josselyn led them into a square room. The thick iron door lock had scorch marks on the metal where someone had forced it open. Musty bolts of material and wooden devices were pressed up against a wall.

"What is this?" Isaac demanded.

Violette hoped Josselyn had a better plan or, at least, a way of distracting the men long enough for her to get the upper hand. Leading them into a useless room was only going to get everyone shot.

Violette tried not to think of Dev freezing in the dining hall. They didn't have time to waste. She scanned the room, assessing the situation.

Josselyn reached for a bolt. Gil stiffened in warning. She held up her hand and then slowly began moving again. "The treasure is here."

Josselyn moved the bolt of material. It activated a mechanism behind the walls. The sound of turning metal creaked and vibrated against the stone. The floor began to slide beneath Gil's feet. His wing twitched, and he automatically tried to fly. However the bound appendage caused his flight pattern to dip sharply to one side, and he stumbled.

Josselyn produced a knife from behind the bolt

and threw it at Gil. The aim was straight, but the sudden dip in Gil's body caused the throw to miss. Violette lunged for Isaac's gun hand. She grabbed his wrist and shifted his weight to heave him toward the ground. The move worked fine practicing with her father's soldiers. Unfortunately, it didn't account for the Corge horn, and she felt the sharp edge of the chipped point snag her snowsuit. Momentum forced it to pierce her skin, cutting her open as he fell.

Violette didn't have time to think about her injury. Josselyn scrambled to get Isaac's gun as it slid across the floor. Gil righted himself, taking aim at Josselyn's back. Violette wasn't sure how it happened, but the next thing she knew she was leaping through the air. Gil fired. The blast struck the top of her shoulder as she pushed Josselyn out of the way. The impact changed her course, sending her flying backward into a wooden frame.

Josselyn screamed, charging Gil. She shoved him into the hole that had opened in the floor. Violette tried to stand. She bled from her shoulder and her side. She crawled for the discarded weapon and lifted it toward Isaac. He still lay on the ground, not moving.

"Violette." Josselyn breathed hard. "You saved me."

Her sister sounded shocked. In truth, Violette

was a little shocked herself. She pushed up from the floor.

Josselyn looked down into the pit. "They told me, but…"

"What is it?" Violette glanced down into the rectangular chamber beneath the room. Steep stone steps led down the side. Bodies had been stacked on the floor, and now only the old bones remained. Gil lay on top of the pile, his lifeless eyes staring up at them. His neck had broken in the fall. Someone had dumped the corpses into the hole in the floor to cover up the crime.

No. Not somebody. Violette knew who was responsible.

"It was the castle treasury, hidden beneath the sewing looms." The sadness in Josselyn's voice was palpable. "Now it's a grave."

Isaac moaned.

"He'll need a medic," Violette said. Her wounds ached. She swayed, a little lightheaded from the blood loss. "We need…Dev."

Josselyn gasped. "You need a medic. I'm sorry. I…" She gestured down and then slid an arm around Violette's back. Yelling, she called, "Jackson? Lucien? Viktor? Rick? Can any of you hear me?"

"Joss?" Lucien yelled. "Where are you? This place is a maze. We heard a shot." The sound of footsteps came and soon Viktor and Lucien were standing before them. "What in all the star blazes happened down here?"

"We were in the tower and lost communication. We came down to find Rick and Jackson unconscious and—who stabbed Violette? Josselyn! Why did you stab Violette?" Viktor instantly went to help support Violette's weight.

"It wasn't me," Josselyn protested.

"Dev," Violette insisted, breathing harder.

"Dev stabbed you?" He frowned, clearly not believing it.

"Evan and Dev are in the dining hall," Josselyn explained. "They don't have snowsuits. Please, hurry. Help them. I've got her."

"I'm on it." Lucien ran from the room.

Viktor looked down into the body dump and then nudged Isaac with his foot. "What about him?"

"We'll contact his ship and have them come for him," Violette answered. Isaac would never forgive her, but she wasn't about to kill him for it.

Viktor pulled out a hand-held medic. "I'll patch him up and keep him sedated, but let me help you first. You're in no condition to walk, let alone run to Dev's side. Lucien will get him. I promise."

Violette grunted as she tugged at her snowsuit. Blood trickled down her arm and side, wetting the black underclothing.

"I'm not a doctor," Viktor warned. "It might not look pretty."

"No sedatives. I'm already lightheaded. Just patch me up." Violette gritted her teeth as he brought the medic to her side to stop the bleeding. The laser burned, but it did its job.

"Thank you, Violette," Josselyn whispered. She didn't have to elaborate.

Violette nodded. In the moment, the choice hadn't been hard. She'd chosen to protect what remained of her family.

Josselyn went to pull the bolt of material to activate the switch to hide the bodies in the floor.

"What were you thinking?" Violette demanded of Josselyn. "Did you think Lucien and Viktor heard us through the broken comms and would come to our rescue?"

"I thought I'd buy some time so we could save ourselves," her sister answered.

Viktor finished his crude doctoring. Her body ached, but Viktor had stopped the bleeding.

"He'll be out for awhile," Viktor said, gesturing toward Isaac. He lifted his hand to his ear.

"What is it?" Violette asked, as she pulled her snowsuit back on. She couldn't hear a faint voice broadcasted on the com like she had with Dev's unit, and figured the brothers had the frequency on a private channel setting due to the attackers.

"Lucien has Dev and Evan. He's getting them out of their shackles and..." Viktor stiffened in horror and looked at Violette. "Go. Run. Dev isn't moving."

Violette hurried as fast as she could, limping her way toward the dining hall. She found Dev unconscious on the floor next to a shivering Evan. Lucien struggled to put his snowsuit back on him. Evan tried to help, but his shaking hands were more of a hindrance and Lucien pushed them out of his way.

"Blast it, Dev, you better not die on me cause I'll spend the rest of my life figuring out how to resurrect your ass so I can tell you that I..." Violette limped to where he lay and collapsed on the stone floor next to him. She breathed hard, focusing past the pain of her injuries. "So I can tell you that I..." Her voice caught, and tears fell over her cheeks. "That I lo—"

"What happened to you? Is that blood?" Evan demanded. His eyes moved to the doorway and Violette knew he worried about his wife.

"Small skirmish. Everyone is whole." Violette pulled off her gloves to help Lucien with Dev's suit.

"Grab the crate. We need to get him out of here," Lucien said. "Dev's internal temperature is naturally hotter and he can't handle a sudden drop in heat."

Violette did as he bid and ran to get the crate with the tapestry. She pushed it over toward them.

"He wanted to get to you, Violette. He'd managed to pull the laser shackles from the floor before collapsing on the ground," Evan told her through shaky lips. His mouth was edged with blue.

"Evan!" Josselyn ran into the room.

"I'm ok," Evan answered. "It's Dev."

"They didn't hurt Rick and Jackson?" Violette asked. She again moved to touch Dev's face, knowing he'd want his friends to be safe.

"We treated them for head wounds, and they were drugged with some manner of heavy sedative. We left them where we found them in a hallway. They could barely walk in a straight line. But, luckily, they were left fully dressed, and haven't suffered much beyond that," Lucien said, before reaching to activate his com to talk to his brother. "Viktor, get the other two and see if you can't help them into a crate for transport. I contacted Lochlann and he is on his way down to fetch us. He'll meet us in the clearing by the gate. The temperature keeps dropping and we need to get out of here."

Violette hooked her arms under Dev's back. Lucien and Josselyn were instantly by her side, helping her lift him into the container. Evan tried to lend a hand by standing beside the crate so it wouldn't slide when they bumped into it. They set Dev down on the tapestry next to the portraits.

"We're never going to get to leave here with treasure, are we?" Lucien said, as they pushed Dev toward the castle entrance. "This place really is cursed."

"There is nothing to come back for," Josselyn said. "The main treasury is empty, and there is nothing but heartache and pain left behind these frozen walls. Unless, you want to come back, Violette?"

"I have my answers. I don't need to revisit." Violette refused to let go of the crate as she kept an eye on Dev's breathing. She reached to touch his cool cheek. "I have all the treasure I want right here."

CHAPTER 23

"IT's NOT FAIR, DEV," Violette stated, not for the first time. "You're not allowed to get out of this relationship by dying. I wasn't kidding when I said I'd séance you back."

He didn't answer her. She wasn't surprised. He hadn't moved for three days.

She sat on the floor of the medical room aboard *The Conqueror* as she waited for the medical booth to finish its current cycle on Dev.

"You have to eat something." Rick stepped into the room and handed her a tray of food. "I can stay with him if you'd like to walk around and stretch your legs."

"I'm not leaving him," Violette denied. She took the tray and set it on the floor. "Thank you, but I'm not hungry."

Rick frowned in disapproval but didn't push the matter. "I was able to confirm that *Racing Banana* picked up Isaac. He's alive. I transmitted those papers you wanted to the pilot, Jo. I think he responded something about finally getting his lady all to himself, but I couldn't get a clear enough signal to hear the entire comment."

"Don't worry about it," Violette answered. "I'm pretty sure I don't want to know."

"What papers?"

Violette gasped at the sound of Dev's raspy voice. She shot up from the floor and rushed to his side. Rick was instantly at the medical booth's system console pressing buttons.

"Dev, you're awake." Violette started to reach in only to stop when she saw the medical lasers at work on his body. "Curse you for scaring me. I thought I lost you."

He gave a weak chuckled. "Um, sorry?"

"I thought you were dying," she accused. "You're never allowed to do that to me again. Do you hear me? I lov—"

"What papers?" he mumbled again.

"I gave Jo the deed to my ship," Violette answered. After what had happened, she really couldn't rejoin her old crew. The ship would cover any back money she owed the pilot plus some. Isaac had forfeited his right to a paycheck when he helped

Gil's insubordination. She'd see to it Ghost got his share of past earnings. "It's just me tying up some loose ends. I'm done with that part of my life. It's time to move forward."

His eyes finally opened. The dark depths peered into hers. She wanted to touch him so badly, but her concern over his health kept her from interfering with the medical booth.

"Dev, about time you got up from your nap, you lazy lophobian," Rick said. The mischief was back in his tone, but she had seen the worry as he checked on his unconscious friend. Winking at Violette, he told her as he walked out the door, "I'm going to tell the others he's awake. Holler if you need me, Vivacious Violette, and I'll come running to your call."

Violette chuckled. "That is one strange man."

"You have no idea," Dev answered. His voice was a little stronger than before. Relief filled her to see his eyes looking at her. She'd been so worried. He lifted his head. "What papers?"

"I told you that I gave Jo the deed to my ship." Violette's relief was short lived as she watched his head drop. "Dev, what's wrong?"

"What papers?" His body jerked violently, and he began to convulse.

"Rick," Violette screamed. She reached her hands into the medical booth and grabbed hold of

Dev's shoulders. His temperature was so hot it nearly burned her fingers. "Rick, something's wrong!"

Rick and Jackson appeared in the doorway.

"Get him out of there," Rick ordered.

"No, wait." Jackson held his hand out to stop Rick from touching the console while at the same time grabbing Violette to pull her away. "He'll be fine. Just, wait…"

Violette struggled to be free. "Something is wrong. He's burning up."

"He's not human," Jackson said. "Not like us. He's only half. Give his body a moment to reset."

Violette felt as if she couldn't breathe. Days of anguish climaxed into this moment. She trembled, helpless to do anything to stop the forceful seizure unfolding in front of her.

"Dev," Violette cried. She elbowed Jackson in the stomach, but the act had little effect. "Let me go, Jackson."

Jackson waited a moment before he released her.

"Dev," Violette rushed to the medical booth. When she touched him, he stopped shaking but didn't open his eyes. She whispered to him, "Dev, listen to me. I love you. I should have said it before now. I've thought it so many times, but I should have said the words. You were right, I was wrong.

What do you need me to say to help you? I'm breaking your curse. I'm earth, or fire, or whatever you need me to be. Just wake up. Please. Open your eyes and wake up. I can't live without you."

"You don't believe in curses," Dev said softly before opening his eyes.

"There you are." Violette caressed his cheek. "Stay with me."

Dev moved inside the booth. "It doesn't look like I have much of a choice. You have me trapped."

Violette slid her hand down his chest. "Your temperature feels like it's returning to normal. How do you feel?" As she said it, she felt the heat from his skin intensify.

"Dev?" Jackson asked from behind her.

"Readings are leveling out," Rick offered from the console.

"Is the ship secure?" Dev asked.

"Yes. Everyone is on board. We're secure." Jackson motioned at Rick. "We'll let everyone know you're awake."

"Did you hear that? I was right. I predicted two for two, Dev and Evan," Rick said as the men left the medical room. "She's the one to break Dev's curse. You all should be coming to me for predictions, not Evan."

Violette continued to stroke Dev's chest.

"I never thought I'd say this out loud, but I think Rick might be right." Dev slid his hand over hers to stop it over his beating heart. "Without you I am cursed, so that must mean—"

"I love you," Violette interrupted. "Did you hear that part? I love you, Devekin. I need to know you heard that. I'm not very good at expressing emotions, but I can become better at it. I love you. I love you. And I hope you love me."

He smiled. "I was trying to tell you I love you, too."

Pleasure filled her.

"There's more." She felt the need to rush and get everything out that she'd been thinking about for the last three days. "I want to marry you and live on this ship, if you can convince the others. I mean, I really don't have anywhere else to go. I gave Jo *Racing Banana*. Josselyn and I are working on a friendship. I don't know that we're all the way there, but I'm trying, and I promise to stop threatening her. I also told her I would do whatever I could to make sure the truth is known about what happened on the Florencian moons. And I love you, Dev. I just love you."

"Violette," Dev tried to reach his hand out, but the booth stopped him. "Can you unlock this contraption now?"

Violette reached for the latch. The lock released,

and Dev stepped out. His naked body radiated heat, and she instantly pressed against him. He wobbled on his feet but was able to stay upright as he leaned against the unit.

He cupped her face. "It's my turn. I'm also not very good at speaking my emotions, but I also want you to hear me. Yes to all of that. I've wanted you in my life since the first time I saw you on Rifflen. You've been in my head, and I think, maybe, there is such a thing as destiny because all the events, over a hundred years' worth, that had to happen to bring us together. I love you, Violette." He gave a helpless gesture. "That's it. I just love you. I never want to let you go."

Violette moaned and lifted up on her toes to press her mouth to his. As it always did with them, primal instinct took over. He swept her up into his arms. Any protest she would have made about his health was lost in his deepening kiss. He strode naked through the ship toward his quarters. No more words were needed between them as bodies pressed together. They had each other, and it was perfection.

The End

THE SERIES CONTINUES...

Space Lords Series
His Frost Maiden
His Fire Maiden
His Metal Maiden
His Earth Maiden
His Woodland Maiden

HIS METAL MAIDEN

A Space Lords Novel

Dragon-shifter Lochlann left home to avoid a war he didn't believe in. Now as Captain of The Conqueror, in charge of a misfit crew, all he wants is to return without the label of coward. He's been offered one chance at redemption: Find Margot, a noblewoman's missing sister. The only problem is, the woman disappeared years ago, and his closest lead is a stunningly beautiful look-a-like droid crafted in her image. Alexis is programed to be everything he could ever desire, but getting her to reveal her secrets proves to be a true challenge for this alpha male.

Being a base model pleasure droid isn't as glamorous as it sounds. Alexis can't remember a time when she wasn't the property of others. Multiple surgeries, and endless tests, have amounted to a life not worth living. When a pirate crew visits her facility, she sneaks onto their ship. Desperate not to be returned to her owners, she strikes a deal with the alluring captain. Pretend to be Margot in exchange for freedom.

Chapter One Excerpt

The Conqueror, Deep Space

"Solar balls and black holes!" Rick ran into the common area of the ship. Breathing hard, he panted, "Alarm. Alarm. Cockpit. Alarm."

Captain Lochlann turned his halfhearted attention toward the pilot. Many of Rick's outbursts were just fits of boredom, or signs of mischief, or, worse, bored mischief that would land them in some intergalactic quagmire. Ever since the pilot had brought a Lintianese curse down on their heads, Lochlann had lost patience for the man's antics.

Lochlann's situation was complicated enough without having his future love life doomed before it began. According to his dragon-shifter people's custom, in order to marry he needed to be on his home planet on their one night of darkness to participate in the breeding ceremony. That wouldn't be such a big deal, except for the fact he was banned from returning to his home planet. Not only couldn't he marry in accordance with his people's beliefs, the chance of finding a woman at all was cursed to fail thanks to Rick's big mouth. Mating was hard enough for dragons. They weren't like other alien cultures. When they married, it was for life. One woman. One wife. One chance at happiness.

"What did you do now, Rick? Asteroids, mine fields, Federation vessels, or ex-girlfriend?" Lochlann drawled, unconcerned. Being in charge of space pirates wasn't something he'd asked for. It just happened. Life was unexpected that way.

Though, to be fair, they weren't *true* space pirates. More like borderline mini-pirates. They didn't follow all the galaxy's laws, but then they didn't attack innocent spaceships and intentionally harm people. They were adventurers—planet-less adventurers—joined together by brotherhood, wanderlust, and a shared need to survive.

"Actually, don't answer. Just fix it." Without indulging whatever Rick was going on about, Lochlann turned back to the game grid before him. Jackson had acquired the new board for Frendle's Chips on their last fuel stop. Metal discs hovered above the grid. Random currents of electricity ran between them in short bursts. The goal was to first sweep the discs out of the grid without getting shocked. Then you had to toss the discs back into place without letting them touch the electricity. Otherwise your disc would turn into particles. The game was popular with serious gamblers, but they were having a hell of a time mastering it.

"There has to be an easier way to win money. Want me to fix it so you never lose?" Viktor was their mechanic and could pretty much rig anything.

"Some of us don't need to cheat to win," Lucien said, mostly to be contrary to his brother. Slender and pale with red-green and red-brown eyes, Viktor and Lucien took after their Dere heritage more than their human side. Irrelevant arguments were pretty much the only way they communicated with each other.

"Cockpit alarm," Rick repeated louder from the doorway when no one gave him the reaction he was looking for. They continued to ignore him.

"No, you're not rigging my board," Jackson asserted. Out of all the current crewmen, he'd been with Lochlann the longest. The man had a secretive military background and, up until very recently, had spent most of his time in the ship's VR room training with his security officer counterpart, Dev. However, since Dev fell in love with Violette Stephans, he didn't have much time for training anymore. Now Jackson was on some strange, almost lonely quest to master every challenge that crossed his path.

Violette's half-sister was also on board. They'd rescued Josselyn Craven from an ice prison, and she'd married the ship's empath, Evan Cormier. Violette and Josselyn weren't the best of friends, and like Viktor and Lucien they bickered if they were left in each other's company for too long. For that reason, he'd encourage their husbands to keep them out of the common area and in their quarters during longer trips.

Maybe arguing was a sibling thing. Lochlann had no idea. He didn't have brothers or sisters.

"We need to do something to earn space credits," Viktor stated. "Our last treasure hunt was a bust, and there is no way I'm ever going back to that abandoned icehole called Florencia's Fifth Moon to search for a third time. My balls still have frostbite."

"That's not frostbite. You have to have balls before they can..." Lucien tried to reach over the active game grid to swipe a disc. Electricity zapped his finger, and he jumped back. Shaking his injured hand, he finished weakly, "be bitten."

"Zenni District," Rick stated, the words softer than before.

That got their attention. All eyes turned toward him.

"Your sex life does not constitute an emergency.

We don't have the space credits to afford a pleasure droid," Lochlann denied the unspoken request. He knew being a single man forced to see two happy couples every day in the close confines of the ship wasn't easy. Sacred cats, he was lonely too. He'd love to buy a pleasure droid to fake companionship on desolate nights. "And we're not burning fuel to go to the Zenni District so that you can walk around and gaze longingly into canister pods in a storage facility."

"We have to go. There's an alarm," Rick insisted.

"What do you keep saying about an alarm?" Jackson frowned. "I have received no security notices."

"Captain Jarek must have set it before he went home. The computers are running a continuous scan for, um, something important," Rick explained ineloquently. "I think in honor of our former captain, we should go to the Zenni District to see about the match the alarm has found."

A zapping noise drew Lochlann's attention back to the game.

Lucien sucked on an injured knuckle and glared at the grid. "You stupid…*game*."

Lochlann missed his captain predecessor. Jarek had been his friend since they were boys shifting and running in the woods of their home planet.

They'd left Qurilixen because they saw no other choice. Lochlann was a Draig dragon-shifter and Jarek was a Var cat-shifting prince. Their people had been at war in some age-old feud that no one understood. The fighting was so ingrained that even during times of peace they still had petty skirmishes. It wasn't like they fought over territory, or social injustice. They just fought because both sides didn't seem to like the other.

Lochlann hadn't wanted to kill anyone. Prince Jarek felt the same. So they left for offworld adventures. Jarek had captained the crew since he was a prince and it was his ship, and Lochlann had been his second in command. Everything had been so new and shiny back then.

But that was years ago. The Draig-Var war had ended, supposedly for good with the death of Jarek's father. Lochlann had his doubts. Peace never seemed to last.

For him, adventures had turned into a way of life, life turned into normal, and now he was no longer Lochlann of the Draig, dragon-shifter exploring space who had a home planet. No, now he was Captain Lochlann of *The Conqueror*, newly in charge of a misfit crew and a traitor on his homeworld for refusing to kill cat-shifters.

Jarek had promoted him before moving home to the Var palace with his wife and infant son. The prince's brothers welcomed him with open arms as if he'd never left. The Draig were not as understanding with Lochlann.

A battle had taken Lochlann's father. Grief killed his mother. He had no siblings. As was the dragon way, others raised him until he was old enough to train for war. He never went hungry, never was without a place to sleep, and had usually been treated kindly, but he was passed from home to home. He'd been a community responsibility.

His youthful decision not to fight didn't go over too well with his people. All he wanted was to remove the label of traitor from his name. He had to restore his honor before he could return home, and the dragon-shifter nobles had given him a way to do just that.

It should have been simple. He had to find one lost human and bring her back to her noblewoman sister. How hard would it be to track one girl? It's not like this Margot was some kind of master criminal. She was a girl from a space fuel dock.

Then why in all the black hole, cursed port, bloody novas could he not complete that one task to find the blasted Margot?

He couldn't even find a trail to follow.

"It's the responsible thing to do," Rick insisted, drawing Lochlann's attention back.

"Is this alarm a sales notification?" Lochlann drawled wryly.

"I don't think Jarek's wife would appreciate his shopping for a pleasure droid," Jackson added.

Lochlann knew for a fact Jarek would never shop for such a thing. He was madly in love with his wife.

"The fact that the pleasure droid manufacturer is located there is not why we're going," Rick said, "but there was an alarm set to go off to let Jarek know, and we need to—"

"I'm thinking Rick may have a point," Viktor interrupted. "And I am in no way basing my opinion on the encoded airwaves Lucien decrypted of the new pleasure droid model advertisements."

"I *am* completely basing my vote on that," Lucien said. "I say Zenni District."

"This is not up for a vote," Lochlann stated. "We're low on space credits, and fuel reserves. It's my job to make sure we make responsible decisions and don't end up floating in the deep black hoping someone reputable rescues our sorry asses."

"What is the alarm for specifically?" Jackson asked.

"Something called a mar-got," Rick said with a shrug.

Lochlann stiffened. "Did you say Margot?"

"What's a Margot?" Jackson asked.

"A girl," Lochlann whispered. It couldn't be. His chest tightened, and he found it hard to breathe.

He missed home. He wanted to see the red dirt and green-tinted skies, to shift into dragon form and run through the shadowed marshes near the border-lands. Instead, he was condemned to the high skies, sailing the deep black looking for a woman who might never be found.

Until now.

Had he finally found Margot?

For a complete, up-to-date booklist, visit
www.MichellePillow.com

ABOUT MICHELLE M. PILLOW

New York Times & *USA TODAY*
Bestselling Author

Michelle loves to travel and try new things, whether it's a paranormal investigation of an old Vaudeville Theatre or climbing Mayan temples in Belize. She believes life is an adventure fueled by copious amounts of coffee.

Newly relocated to the American South, Michelle is involved in various film and documentary projects with her talented director husband. She is mom to a fantastic artist. And she's managed by a dog and cat who make sure she's meeting her deadlines.

For the most part she can be found wearing pajama pants and working in her office. There may or may not be dancing. It's all part of the creative process.

Come say hello! Michelle loves talking with readers on social media!

www.MichellePillow.com

f facebook.com/AuthorMichellePillow

X x.com/michellepillow

⊙ instagram.com/michellempillow

BB bookbub.com/authors/michelle-m-pillow

g goodreads.com/Michelle_Pillow

a amazon.com/author/michellepillow

▶ youtube.com/michellepillow

P pinterest.com/michellepillow

COMPLIMENTARY EXCERPTS

TRY BEFORE YOU BUY!

THE SAVAGE KING

BY MICHELLE M. PILLOW

Curious to see the Var side of things?

Lords of the Var® Book One
by Michelle M. Pillow

A Qurilixen World Novel

Bestselling Cat-shifter Romance Series

Cat-shifting King Kirill knows he must do his duty by his people. When his father unexpectedly dies, it's his destiny to take the throne and all of the responsibility that entails. What he hadn't prepared for is the troublesome prisoner that's now his to deal with.

Undercover Agent Ulyssa is no man's captive.

Trapped in a primitive forest awaiting pickup, she's going to make the best out of a bad situation... which doesn't include falling for the seductions of a king.

About *Lords of the Var*® (Books 1-5)

You met their father, King Attor, in Dragon Lords Books 1-4, now meet the Var Princes!

The cat-shifter princes were raised to not believe in love, especially love for one woman, and they will do everything in their power to live up to their father's expectations. Oh, how the mighty will fall.

The Savage King Excerpt

Kirill watched the door to his bedroom open. He'd been sitting in the dark, trying to relieve the stress headache that had built behind his eyes for the last week. The pain started at the base of his skull and radiated up to his temples until he could hardly see straight.

A heavy responsibility had been thrust on his shoulders, a responsibility he really hadn't prepared

himself for, the welfare of the Var people. King
Attor had not left him in a good position. He'd
rallied the people to the brink of war, convinced
them that the Draig were their enemy, and even
went so far as to attack the Draig royal family.

Kirill wanted to see peace in the land. However,
he knew the facts didn't bode well for it. The Draig
had a long list of grievances against King Attor and
the Var kingdom.

Before his death, the king had ordered an attack
on the four Draig princes, all of which ended
horribly for the Var. The worst was when Prince
Yusef was stabbed in the back, a most cowardly
embarrassment for the Var guard who did it. If he
hadn't been executed in the Draig prisons, he
would've been ostracized from the Var community.
Luckily, Prince Yusef survived or they'd already be
at battle.

Attor had also arranged for the kidnapping of
Yusef's new bride. The Draig Princess Olena had
been rescued, or that too would've led to war. The
old king had even tried to poison Princess Morri-
gan, the future Draig queen, on two separate occasions. She too lived. And those were only a few of
the offenses Kirill knew about in the few weeks
before King Attor's death. He could just imagine
what he didn't know.

Kirill sighed, feeling very tired. He'd known

since birth that the day would come when he'd be expected to step up and lead the Var as their new king. He just hadn't expected it to be for another hundred or so years. His father had been a hard man, whom he'd foolishly believed was invincible.

"Here kitty, kitty, kitty." His lovely houseguest's whisper drew his complete attention from his heavy thoughts.

Ulyssa bent over like she expected him to answer to the insulting call. He dropped his fingers from his temple into his lap, and a quizzical smile came to his lips. As he watched her, he wasn't sure if he was angered or amused by her words.

"Are you in here, you little furball?" she said, a little louder.

She wore his clothes. Never had the outfit looked sexier. His jaw tightened in masculine interest, as he unabashedly looked her over. All too well did he remember the softness of her body against his and the gentle, offering pleasure of her sweet lips. She'd made soft whimpering noises when he'd touched her, yielding, purring sounds in the back of her throat. Even with the aid of nef, he was surprised by how easily and confidently she melted into him. The Var were wild, passionate people and were drawn to the same qualities in others. He suspected she'd be an untamed lover.

Too bad she'd belonged to his father first. In his

mind, that made her completely untouchable though none would dare question his claim if he were to take her to his bed. Technically, by Var law, she belonged to him until he chose to release her. For an insane moment, he thought about keeping her as a lover. He knew he wouldn't, but the thought was entertaining.

Kirill's grin deepened. Ulyssa strode across his home to the bathroom door with an irritated scowl. It was obvious she didn't see him in the darkened corner, watching her. He detected her engaging smell from across the room, the smell of a woman's desire. It stirred his blood, making his limbs heavy with arousal. And, for the first time since his father's death, his headache relieved itself.

"Hum, maybe I'm looking too high. I'm sure there has to be a little cat door here somewhere. Come here, little kitty. Where are you hiding?"

His slight smile fell at her words. It was easy to detect her mocking tone.

"Where's your little kitty door, huh?" Ulyssa whispered to herself, her blue gaze searching around in the dark.

Kirill grimaced in further displeasure. He watched her open the door to his weapons cabinet. Her eyes rounded, and he thought she might take one. She didn't. Instead, she nodded in appreciation before closing the door and continuing her search for an exit.

She stopped at a narrow window by his kitchen doorway. Her neck craned to the side, as she tried to see out over the distance. Kirill knew she looked at the forest. From under her breath, he heard her vehement whisper, "Where exactly did you little fur balls bring me? Ugh, I need to get out of this flea trap, even if I have to fight every one of you cowardly felines to do it. I've fought species twice as big and three times as frightening. A couple of little kitty cats don't scare me."

If this insolent woman wanted to play tough, oh, he'd play. Curling gracefully forward, Kirill shifted before his hands even touched the ground. He let one thick paw land silently on the floor, followed by a second. Short black fur rippled over his tanned flesh, blending him into the shadows. His clothes fell from his body, and he lowered his head as he crept forward. A low sound of warning started in the back of his throat. He was livid.

**To find out more about Michelle's books
visit www.MichellePillow.com**

PLEASE LEAVE A REVIEW

THANK YOU FOR READING!

Please take a moment to share your thoughts by leaving a review.

Be sure to check out Michelle's other titles at

www.michellepillow.com

www.ingramcontent.com/pod-product-compliance
Lightning Source LLC
Chambersburg PA
CBHW020912130726
47904CB00006BA/1841